Praise for

Frances and Bernard

New York Times Book Review Editors' Choice • Indie Next List Pick • BN.com Staff Pick for February • An Amazon Best Book of the Month • Historical Novel Society Editors' Choice

"Incandescent ... A wholly original, fully fleshed, sparklingly alive, thrilling, moving, jam-packed epistolary novel of a mere 208 pages ... Their connection feels so profound, electric, and real that it's hard to believe Bauer didn't copy verbatim actual missives between Flannery O'Connor and Robert Lowell ... I finished this novel in tears, not at all ready to have it end, but with the satisfied, enthralled sense that it had accomplished exactly, perfectly, what it needed to."

— *Elle*

"Bauer is ... a distinctive stylist who can write about Simone Weil or Kierkegaard with wit and charm. A fresh voice thinking seriously about what a religiously committed life might have felt like and per-haps, in our own far-from-tranquil period, might feel like again."

— *New York Times Book Review*

"A moving tale about kindred spirits ... The book showcases an era in which literature and intellect were celebrated; its epistolary form lends itself to a delightful exchange of ideas as the protagonists dance with the possibility of love — and face its disappointments.★★★"

— *People*

"Bauer writes with authority and gusto about issues of faith ... The big questions are still worth asking."

— *Washington Post*

"Graceful and gem-like . . . Through Bauer's sharp, witty, and elegant prose, [Frances and Bernard] become vibrant and original characters . . . After finishing this sweet and somber novel, we might sigh and think, 'It's a shame we don't write love letters anymore' — before stopping for a moment to marvel at the subtlety of what Bauer has wrought out of history and a generous imagination, and being thankful that someone still is." — *Boston Globe*

"In her lively, intelligent new novel, Bauer creates two characters who are so present on the page, we seem to be eavesdropping on their conversation . . . Their letters dance and sparkle with the passion of two minds delighting in each other . . . A small gem, reflecting the rare joy of finding someone who is, quixotically, counterintuitively and completely, yours." — *More*

"The writing has moments of quietly bracing insight, as these two fiercely particular individuals attempt to navigate the other." — *New York Times*

"[Bauer] imagines the relationship that might have been, and readers can happily indulge in both a well-written, compelling love story and, if they're anything like us, a little bit of romantic wish-fulfillment for one of their favorite authors." — *Atlantic*

"Our fave new novel . . . You'll laugh and cry as two writers back in the 1950s forge an unlikely friendship — and romance — by sending oh-so-beautifully-written letters to each other." — *Self*

"Bauer's characters are entirely her own. The beautifully imagined correspondence, spanning a decade, ranges over themes of love, creativity, and suffering." — *Martha Stewart's Whole Living*

"Blooming with richness and intelligence . . . These two voices in Bauer's fine rendering sing counterpoint that is exhilarating and heartbreaking . . . Their relation stirs into the love, for each, of a lifetime. A marvelous tracing of these lives."

— *Buffalo News*

"With wonderful writing, elegant, pithy and witty, the author reeled me in from the very beginning . . . [*Frances and Bernard*] wrestle[s] with big questions in gorgeous and sharply hewn language. There is much to admire in this smart, ambitious debut novel."

— *Pittsburgh Post-Gazette*

"A novel of stunning subtlety, grace, and depth . . . compos[ed in] dueling letters of breathtaking wit, seduction, and heartbreak."

— *Booklist,* **starred review**

"Engrossing . . . Funny, sweet and sad. A lovely surprise."

— *Publishers Weekly,* **starred review**

"A beautiful book, made for people who like both intelligent conversation and romance (we are legion). But Bauer's true accomplishment is not the loveliness of the prose but rather the kindness of her intentions. O'Connor died of lupus at age forty and never married, but the fictional Frances experiences true love in her stead — and may even get a happy ending."

— *Coffin Factory*

"Thanks to Bauer's sharply honed writing chops, Lowell and O'Connor come to sparkling life in a love story that will have you shaking your head and saying, 'Dang I wish I'd known these two!'"

— **AARP**

"A pleasure ... [Bauer] writes about writing and faith with talent approaching that of her two models." — *Las Vegas Weekly*

"[*Frances and Bernard*] is heartbreaking in all the right ways ... Recommended if: you love *Mad Men* but wish it were a little more romantic." — **Radio.com**

"Fluid, rich writing and vivid characterisations ... [*Frances and Bernard*] made me smile all the way through as though a beloved friend has been resurrected to entertain, instruct and beguile me." — *Australian*

"Wielding humor and a marvelous sense of understatement ... [Bauer] bring[s] credible voices and superb moments to these two characters destined to be talented writers in full ascendance on the New York literary scene of the 1960s ... A novel about love and faith that shows a grace that is nearly miraculous." — *Le Monde*

"Irresistible." — *Daily Mail*

"A wholly original, very moving novel about how sometimes the deepest relationships in our lives are also the most impossible. My eyes filled with tears. It is wonderful to read something so rare and true. What a rich writer and two unforgettable lovers!"
— **Stephanie Cowell, author of *Claude and Camille: A Novel of Monet* and *The Physician of London***

"I did not merely love Frances and Bernard; I worried myself sick over them. And the prose! So delectable you could eat it for dessert."
— **Monica Wood, author of *When We Were the Kennedys* and *Any Bitter Thing***

"A terrific narrative [with] emotional force. Bauer recaptures a time in which people took one another more seriously, an era when they still inclined toward epistolary explorations instead of self-promoting tweets. *Frances and Bernard* is one of the best first novels I've read in years." — **Thomas Mallon, author of *Watergate* and *Henry and Clara***

"There are so many reasons to love this perfect novel, not least because before our eyes Bauer quietly reveals the lovers to each other, and to themselves, while she explores all of the important problems of faith, work, art, marriage, passion, and how best to lead the life that you think you're meant to live. *Frances and Bernard* is smart and clear and deep and beautiful. I worship it."

— **Jane Hamilton, author of *Disobedience, A Map of the World,* and *The Book of Ruth***

"I'll never stop raving about *Frances and Bernard*. I loved, admired and devoured it; didn't want it to end. Dear, brilliant, and unforgettable." — **Elinor Lipman, author of *Family Man***

"Dazzling and gorgeously written, *Frances and Bernard* features a pair of brilliant, complicated writers who present themselves to each other in letters that form the most exciting epistolary novel in recent memory. A slim book, it still seems to say all of the important things about friendship, faith, love, the literary life, and especially the costs of living as an artist while still inhabiting the real world. It's a marvel."

— **Ann Packer, author of *The Dive from Clausen's Pier* and *Songs Without Words***

ALSO BY CARLENE BAUER

Not That Kind of Girl: A Memoir

Frances
and
Bernard

CARLENE BAUER

Mariner Books
Houghton Mifflin Harcourt
BOSTON • NEW YORK

First Mariner Books edition 2014

For information about permission to reproduce selections from this book,
write to Permissions, Houghton Mifflin Harcourt Publishing Company,
215 Park Avenue South, New York, New York 10003.

www.hmhco.com

Library of Congress Cataloging-in-Publication Data
Bauer, Carlene.
Frances and Bernard / Carlene Bauer.
p. cm.
ISBN 978-0-547-85824-1 (hardback)   ISBN 978-0-544-10517-1 (pbk.)
1. Authors — Fiction.
2. New York (N.Y.) — Social life and customs — 20th century — Fiction. I. Title.
PS3602.A934F73 2012
813'.6 — dc23
2012014028

Book design by Brian Moore

Printed in the United States of America
DOC 10 9 8 7 6 5 4 3 2 1

For
Anna Mae Bauer

So, I have written you a love letter, oh, my God, what have I done!

— Fyodor Dostoevsky, *The Brothers Karamazov*

Dearest Claire —

How are you?

Here I am in Philadelphia, back from the colony. It was mildly horrific, except for the writing. I finished what I think might be a draft of the novel. If I can just figure out a way to continuously sponge off the rich, the rest of my life should go very well!

I fear, however, that I will have to become a teacher to support this habit. I don't think the rich found me very grateful, and they probably won't ask me back to their glen. Oh well.

And now I will tell you the mildly horrific part. You deserved a honeymoon, but the whole time I was there I kept wishing that you could have come with me so that we could have taken long walks together fellowshipping in daily indictment of our fellow guests. Here were my spiritual exercises: I prayed, and then I had conversations with you in my head about the idiotic but apparently talented. I kept silent at meals, mostly, and this silence, as I hoped, kept people from trying to engage with me. I had nothing to say to them, because they were always telling stories about the other writers they knew or the hilarious things they'd gotten up to while drinking. And me, dry as the town of Ocean Grove. Sample colonists: Two poets, boys, our age. Editors at two different literary magazines. Indistinguishable. Their names do not bear repeating. Sample dinner story: These two had been members of a secret society at Yale, with one the head and the other his deputy. The head would sit on a gold-painted throne they'd stolen from the drama department to interview potential candidates. "Sodomy or disembowelment," he'd ask, "and every man who answered *disembowelment* got in." And then this, from the cocktail party they threw for us the first night: A novelist (a lady novelist, a writer of historical romances). Your mother has probably read them. I've seen them eaten with peanuts on trains. Was introduced to her as a fellow novelist and that was the last she cared to know of me, as she was off on a monologue detailing her busy reading and lecture schedule; the difficulties of balancing this schedule and her writing; the infinite patience of her advertising-executive husband, who never minds using his vacation time to travel to Scotland and Ireland and France for her research; the infinite patience of her dear, dear editor, who always picks up the phone when she needs to be cajoled out of an impasse, which isn't often. "Thank heavens I'm a visceral writer. It just comes out of me in a flood. I can't stop it. I usually need about three weeks here for six hundred pages, which I then whittle down to a —" I wanted so badly to tell her what this self-centered harangue was making my viscera do. Sometimes there's no more satisfactory oath to utter at these times but an exasperated *Jesus Christ.* I'd feel bad about taking the Lord's name in vain but I like to think he's much more offended by the arrogance that drives me to offer up such a bitterly desperate beseechment. Well, I guess he's offended by my bitterness too, but — a visceral writer. Dear God. Claire, please let me never describe myself or my work with such conviction. The self-regard that fuels so many — I will never get over it. It's like driving drunk, it seems to me. Although these people never kill anybody — they just blindside everyone until they've cleared a path to remunerative mediocrity.

On the few occasions I did speak at these gatherings, I was looked at as if I were a child of three who'd toddled up to their elbows, opened her mouth, and started speaking in perfect French. I enjoyed that. Silence, exile, cunning.

There was one young man who did bear scrutiny. Bernard Eliot. Harvard. Descended from Puritans, he claims. Another poet. But very good. Well, I guess I should say more than *very good*. Great? I know nothing about poetry, except that I either like it or don't. And his I liked very much. I hear John Donne in the poems — John Donne prowling around in the boiler room of them, shouting, clanging on pipes with wrenches, trying to get this young man to uncram the lines and cut the poems in half. We had a nice lunch one day — he asked me to lunch, he said, because he'd noticed me reading a book by Etienne Gilson. He converted a few years ago. Here I frown: could be a sign of delusions of grandeur, when a Puritan turns to Rome. He said an astounding thing at lunch. He asked me if I had a suitor — his word — and I said no. I was pretty sure this was just to start conversation. Then, after a pause, while I was shaking some ketchup out over my french fries, he said, chin in hand, as if he were speaking to me from within some dream he was having, "I think men have a tendency to wreck beautiful things." I wanted to laugh. I couldn't figure out what kind of response he wanted — was he trying to determine if I was the kind of girl who had experience with that kind of wreckage and who would then be a willing audience for a confession of some of his own, or was he laying a flirtatious trap to see how much of his own wreckage I'd abide? Instead I asked him if he wanted the ketchup. "Actually, yes, thanks," he said, and then, while shaking it out over his own fries, "Have you ever been to Italy?" He asked if he could write me while he was there. I did like him. Though I think he comes from money, and has read more at twenty-five than I will have read by the time of my death, he seemed blessedly free of pretension. Grandiose statements about romance notwithstanding.

Tell me of Paris. Send my love to Bill. When can I visit you in Chicago?

Love,
Frances

Dear Ted —

I'm packing for Italy, and sorry that I won't get a chance to see you before I leave and you come back from Maine. Say hello to your mother and father for me. Will you finally make a conquest of that lobsterman's daughter? I think you're making this effort only to weave a line about it into the final ballad of Ted McCoy, just so your sons and grandsons have something to which they might aspire. Which I applaud. It's as good as catching a mermaid.

It's a damn shame that you didn't get accepted to the colony. I've said it before and there, I said it again. They decided to give all the fiction spots to women this round. Everyone there was a thoroughgoing hack. There was a pert, kimono-wearing Katherine Mansfield type to flirt with, but she wasn't smart enough to consider doing anything serious about. Which was all for the best. She couldn't remember my name until the second week of our stay. She insisted on calling me Anton. "I'm sorry, you remind me of —" but she would never say who this Anton was. I wanted to know! She meant to give off an air of mystery — instead she gave off an air of distracted imbecility.

I met a girl I quite liked — but not in that way. I think you'd like her too. She looks untouched, as if she grew up on a dairy farm, but she's dry, quick, and quick to skewer, so there's no mistaking that she was raised in a city. Philadelphia. Her name is Frances Reardon. Was a little Mother Superiorish. She's just escaped from the workshop at Iowa. She was the only other real writer there. Her novel is about a hard-hearted nun who finds herself receiving stigmata. It sounds juvenile, but it's very funny. (I stole a look at some pages in her bag at lunch when she'd gone to get us some coffee.) Clearly someone educated by bovine-minded Catholics taking her revenge — but for God. A curious mix of feminine and unfeminine — wore a very conventional white dress covered in the smallest of brown flowers and laid her napkin down on her lap with something approaching fussiness, but then thumped the bottom of a ketchup bottle as if she were pile driving. At one point said that "reading the verse of Miss Emily Dickinson makes me feel like I'm being suffocated by a powder puff full of talc" but avowed that she did like Whitman. "Does that give me the soul of a tramp?" she said, smiling. Very charming, and without meaning to be. A rare thing. Also a very, very good writer. She made me laugh quite a bit. And yet she is religious. Also very rare. I think I might try to make her a friend.

I know you're not a letter writer, but drop me a postcard or two.

Yours,
Bernard

September 20, 1957

Dear Frances —

I hope this letter finds you well and still pleasurably hard at work.

I write to you from outside Florence, Italy, where an old professor of mine has a family house that he has very kindly allowed me to come and stay in. I'm finishing my book here.

I very much enjoyed talking with you this summer, and I would like to talk to you some more. But I'm in Italy. And you're in Philadelphia. So will you talk to me in letters?

Have you ever been to Italy? In Italy, I feel musical and indolent. All speech is arpeggio.

I wanted to ask you this question when we had lunch: Who is the Holy Spirit to you?

Sincerely,
Bernard

Dear Bernard —

I was so very pleased to receive your note. Thank you for writing me. It would be a pleasure to talk to you in letters.

I have not been to Italy, but I have been to London, where I remember seeing young Italian tourists thronging about major landmarks and chattering in a way that made me think of pigeons. I know that must be unfair, but that is my only impression of Italy, refracted as it is through the prism of stodgy old England.

Have you ever been to Philadelphia? Right now, as summer winds down, it is fuzzy with heat and humidity, and the scent of the sun baking the bricks of the houses in this neighborhood. I feel indolent, but not musical. I am waitressing while I try to find a job in New York. One that allows me to pay the rent without taxing my brain. I can be a night owl and wouldn't mind writing until the wee hours after work.

The Holy Spirit! Bernard, you waste no time. I believe he is grace and wisdom.

I hope your work is going well.

Sincerely,
Frances

October 30, 1957

Dear Frances —

There are pigeons here too. These Italian boys hoot and coo at the young foreign women wandering through the piazzas. Both sides are intractable — the boys with their intense conviction that they can catch something this way, the girls in their perturbation, their furrowed brows. It gives me great pleasure to sit and watch this. I keep hoping that one of these days a girl will whirl around and take one up on his invitation.

I've never been to Philadelphia.

I don't believe in wasting time when I've met someone I want to know more of.

I don't know what the Holy Spirit is or does. I think this is because I came to Catholicism late and have felt hesitant to penetrate this mystery. Protestants shove the Holy Spirit to the side — too mystical, too much a distraction from the Father and Son. They regard the Holy Spirit with the same suspicion, I think, as they do the saints — it's a form of idolatry to shift the focus to a third party, whether it be the Holy Spirit or Saint Francis. To appeal to the third party is pagan. Is he grace and wisdom? How do you know?

Let's not ever talk of work in these letters. When I see you again I want to talk to you about work, but I am envisioning our correspondence as a spiritual dialogue.

Sincerely,
Bernard

November 20, 1957

Dear Bernard —

Deal. No discussion of work. I don't like to write about the writing either. I can talk about it, if pressed, but I prefer silence. I don't want to be responsible for any pronouncements on which I might fail to follow through.

I have to tell you — I am wary of projects that are described as spiritual. I fear — this is related to my aversion to artistic empty threats — that the more consciously spiritual a person appears to be, the less truly spiritual that person is. I know what you're after isn't that at all. Perhaps what I am also wary of is the notion that enough dogged inquiry will induce enlightenment. It may be a mistake to think that it can.

This is also why I fear I can't talk about the Holy Spirit in a way that will make him visible or present to you. I believe that he is counsel, because that is how Christ described him. To me *counsel* means that he is grace and wisdom. But I've never experienced grace and wisdom hovering like a flame over my head, and if I do ever realize that I acted wisely or received foresight clearly because of the Holy Spirit, I will let you know. But I don't ever want to feel touched or gifted spiritually. Or sense God moving about on the face of my waters. What a burden! Everything would then have to live up to being knocked off a horse by lightning, wouldn't it? I think I prefer to live at the level of what the British call *muddle*. Muddle with occasional squinting at something that might be called clarity in the distance, so as not to despair.

Sincerely,
Frances

December 6, 1957

Dear Frances —

Points taken. My enthusiasm over finding someone with whom to talk these things over got the better of me.

My sin is poetizing. Can you tell?

As much as you protest, I think I have a better understanding now of the H.S.

Why do you despair?

Italy has ceased to be musical. It now feels decrepit and entombing, and I'm glad to be leaving next week. I'm not even taking pleasure in the fact that my Italian is now as musical as my German is serviceable. I don't feel indolent anymore either; I feel crushed by effort. I feel that I'm toting slabs of marble around from second guess to second guess.

I have sinned against us — I have spoken of work. Give me a penance.

When I come back I'll be living in Boston with Ted, a friend of mine — a college roommate whom I call my brother. I'm going to be teaching some classes at Harvard. I'll also be the editor of the *Charles Review*. I am looking forward to being back in Boston. I'm not looking forward to being that close again to my parents, but I think I can keep their genteel philistinism at bay. Send me your next letter at the address on the back of this page.

In fact, send me some of that novel you're working on. I command you.

Yours,
Bernard

December 15, 1957

Bernard —

Please enjoy this postcard depicting Philadelphia's storied art museum and the mighty Schuylkill. Now you do not ever have to visit.

I hope that you are settling down in Boston. I hope that your marble slabs have become fleshly and alive again.

Oh, I don't despair of anything. At least right now. I was being hyperbolic. If I did despair, I probably wouldn't tell you of it, for your sake and mine! And God's. If I described my despair I would be poetizing and legitimizing it. And I'm not Dostoevsky.

I won't send you some of the novel just yet — it is still percolating. But I am flattered that you want to see it at all.

Penances are God's purview, not mine. Instead, I will wish you a merry Christmas. Love and joy come to you, and to your wassail too.

Sincerely,
Frances

Dear Frances —

Happy new year! It is 1958. Do you care?

I have turned my book in. Now I am in that terrible period between labors, waiting for editorial orders, pacing the apartment like Hamlet waiting for his father's ghost. Although I have begun to write what may be poems for the next one, I can't throw myself into them quite yet. The lines are an insubordinate gang of children who have sized their father up and found him feckless. The only thing to do with this restlessness is talk and drink. Or box. I went to a gym a few times when I was at Harvard, thinking I would take it up, but I quickly abandoned that scheme. "Did you forget your bloomers?" a gentleman once said to me while we were sparring. I knocked him flat and never went back, knowing that I would have wanted to punch me, too, had I been a regular and spied my Ivied, ivory self sauntering through the door. If I didn't have to teach in a few days, and I keep forgetting that I do, I would probably get on a bus or a plane and hope to be invigorated by foreign context. I thought I had tired of Italy, but now — in frigid, colorless Boston, clouds like lesions, having had a dispiriting dinner with my parents, museum pieces already, immobilized by their complacencies — I wish I were there again, where history hung in the air like incense after a Mass, still alive, where around every corner there lurked a spiritual or architectural delight.

Here is a delight: the prospect of getting to know you better. To that end:

Frances, where in this world have you been besides London?

Where in this world would you like to go?

Have you been reading anything you like? Anything you *loathe?*

What is your confirmation name, and why?

The gospels or Paul?

Or is that the wrong question entirely?

Paradise Lost or *The Divine Comedy*? Or neither, and instead the whole of Shakespeare?

Or is that the wrong question entirely?

James Baldwin? (Say yes.)

Gossip — in the hierarchy of sins, I'd put it a step or two below venial, wouldn't you?

Whose food did you most want to poison at the colony?

Have you ever sent a letter you wish you hadn't?

Or forget all that and — tell me something I might not believe about you.

Yours,
Bernard

January 10, 1958

Dear Bernard —

Although I have yet to turn a book in to a publisher myself, I have a feeling I would experience something very similar. I have been known, at the end of a school year, to spend a good two weeks feeling that if I did not have an exam to take or a paper to write, there was no reason for me to be alive. I get the existential shakes — I'm like one of those small metal wind-up toys that chatter in circles until they peter out, exhausted, and finally keel over. When my existential shakes peter out — gradually I comprehend that no one's going to phone me at home asking for a twenty-page paper by next Thursday — I can go down the shore with a clear conscience.

Whom did *you* want to poison at the colony?

Something you might not believe about me? Hmmm. I'm not sure that we've known each other long enough to have ideas about what in our characters would prove contradictory! Hmmm. You might not believe that children like me, but they do. Or that I have not been able to stop playing *Ella and Louis Again* since I received it for Christmas. I feel ill-equipped to discuss just what it is I love in that record — I am the epitome of square, and I know nothing about music — but there is something about the lower register of her voice that makes me feel as if I am afloat in an ocean the color of midnight.

I think writing to a poet may be rubbing off on me, and not for the good.

Here's something else. I had a girlhood crush on Cary Grant. I was not the kind of girl who had crushes on movie stars — that was my sister, who had a framed picture of Tyrone Power on her dresser. But Grant seemed like someone out of a novel rather than a creature cobbled together on a studio lot. What is it? He is refined but also given to the ridiculous, and the ridiculousness never erases his refinement. Well, I shouldn't lie. I still have a girlhood crush on Cary Grant. He may be the cement in my relationship with my aunt Peggy. She will say aloud from behind the paper, as if she means to invite everyone in the room and not just me, "*An Affair to Remember* is playing up over at the Ritz," and I will say, with feigned nonchalance from behind my book, "What time?" and then we will race out of the house like women who've been told he will be there in the flesh.

Both the gospels *and* Paul; the gospels because they represent God's faith in our imagination, and Paul because more often than not we are too stupid to use it.

And now you have heard more than enough from me. Please do write soon.

Sincerely,
Frances

January 17, 1958

Dear Frances —

Let us settle this once and for all: *I* am the epitome of square. In fact, the other day a group of students lovingly accused me of this when they found out I did not own jazz records. I don't, and I'll tell you why: it is an agent of agitation, and I'm already agitated enough. It's not that I don't like jazz. I wish I could. It's just that one song is the equivalent of four dozen phone calls to a switchboard that's already buzzing and sparking like a pinball machine. I'm ten years younger than Kerouac, and yet the response to his book makes me feel that my shirts are as starched as my father's. Kerouac and I are Catholics, and yet I cringe at his ecstasies: there is nothing revealed by his mysticism but his own psychology. The self-taught always do make me a little impatient because they make idolatries of their heroes, or of their own psyches, that suspend them in artistic adolescence. Lorraine, the kimonoed odalisque whom you may remember from the colony, is an exemplar of this type, with her worship of Colette. I'm not jealous of Kerouac, or perplexed by him — just indifferent. To my students' chagrin. I think they want me to launch into a philippic declaiming him as a false heir to Rome — want some kind of reactionary grandstanding intellectual contretemps played out in front of them. They also want me to give them permission to behave badly because they are writing poems. I have behaved badly, but it wasn't because I thought my gift needed to be fed by it. The most talented students this year think that talent absolves them from discipline. Since none of this talent is large enough to make me feel I need to rescue them from this folly, I sit back and watch them bark and loaf as if they were seals on the rocks in Maine. What do I care? I just finished a book; I'm glad of the vacation. I am now writing every day, and I'd rather not have many other demands made on me.

I'm no moviegoer, but even I can tell Cary Grant is gifted with an obscene amount of elegance — however, I would never have taken you for a fan of anything remotely related to jazz. Although now that I think about it, there is something in you, I believe, that swings. It manifests in your smile.

Children like me too. I intuit that they take me for a bear.

Whom I would have poisoned: that woman who was cannibalizing *Ivanhoe*! She reminded me a little of my mother.

Here's a gift for you. I remember you said that you liked Bach, that day we had lunch at the colony. I am sending you this recording of Glenn Gould, which I think you might like quite a bit. (It's come to this, as I near the end of my third decade: I prefer my angry young men angry with Chopin.) I am particularly enamored of #25.

Yours,
Bernard

January 24, 1958

Dear Bernard —

Thank you so very much for the record. What a lovely gift. I put it on the evening I received it and found myself laying my book aside and just listening. And I've been listening to it ever since. It's like nothing else.

Oh, I remember Lorraine.

Regarding Kerouac, I'm allergic too. The Beats are really nothing more than a troop of malevolent Boy Scouts trying to earn badges for cultural arson. Ahem. To your point about feeling as starched as your father, I say: Why don't I just take up knitting already? I feel compelled to stress that I always voted for Democrats.

About being self-taught — I'd say that I was self-taught compared to you, being as I was educated by parochial-school nuns and graduated from a college that was not Harvard. But I never have made heroes of writers, so maybe that's why you're still writing me.

Other than the Gould, which made me forget we were in the dead of January, I have no news! No anecdotes! I write, I work, I cook, I read in the living room while my father does a crossword puzzle and my sister washes the dishes, and then I retire to my chamber when they turn the television on. To me, the dead of January is to be as feared as the ides of March. But I would like to make a formal request. Would you tell me how you converted? It is something I have been wanting to hear.

Again, thank you for the record.

Yours,
Frances

January 31, 1958

Dear Frances —

I'm still writing you because I want your friendship, silly girl. I didn't mean to hurt your feelings. I can see where you might characterize yourself as self-taught — from what I can tell, whatever you learned, you learned in spite of your schooling, not because of it — but I'm speaking of the intellectually feral. What I have observed is that you have respect for tradition while not being weighed down by it. You know what you like and who you'll follow, and when and why and where you'll part ways. Most of the writers I admire possess this combination of reverence and courage. If you don't know anything, I tell my students, you at least need to know the rules. But I forget how much trouble I was as a student. I was hellishly belligerent. I once made a young professor of German cry because she refused to accept poems I'd written (in German) as a final exam. I told her that her fanatical adherence to protocol made her a stereotype, which made her a poor ambassador for her country, which needed all the good publicity it could get.

I really didn't mean to hurt your feelings.

The dead of winter is a terrible thing. Ted and I are throwing a party this weekend to try to distract ourselves from how terrible it truly is. He has just come up to me with a tray full of shot glasses that contain various iterations of a bloody mary he is trying to perfect, and I have been telling him that they all taste like spiked canned soup. Ted says hello. He adds that you should not listen to me on matters of taste, because I have been known to subsist for days on nothing but peanuts and beer, like an alcoholic circus elephant.

I'll write to you of my conversion in my next letter. I am in no mood to fulminate on paper — I wish the two of us were in a room together talking of what matters most, the air thick with affinity. In January a man crawls into a cave of hopelessness; he hallucinates sympathies catching fire. Letters are glaciers, null frigates, trapping us where we are in the moment, unable to carry us on toward truth.

Yours,
Bernard

February 11, 1958

Dear Bernard —

No apologies needed. I thought what I had written was a wink, but I can see what I might have sounded like. Even though you're making a guess based on one long lunch, I think you may be right about me. I have taken what I needed from Miss Austen and some Russians and I have packed my bags.

Was your party a success? Did Ted realize that he needed to add mustard powder to his bloody marys?

Bernard, that poor German professor! My aunts liked to say I had the devil in me, but they would have gone right ahead and called in a priest to exorcise you. Now, remind me again — do you *like* women or do you *loathe* them? Just so I know how to proceed.

Well, I will keep this letter very short. I have to review two books for Iowa's journal and I need to take a pile of notes on them. Here is a sneak preview of my review: If one is going to write of a crisis of faith, do not ask the reader to believe that the crisis can be solved only by (a) marriage, or (b) suicide.

Before I go — I know what you mean about letters vs. rooms. Christ would not have taught the disciples by correspondence course, I'm fairly sure.

Yours,
Frances

February 23, 1958

Dear Frances —

My, you do chide. But I like it.

You asked me to tell you how I converted.

As a child, I was taken to a Congregationalist church. We went roughly every week — and by *we,* I mean my mother and myself. It meant nothing, really, it was just what was done. My father, I think, thought it my mother's job to take me. I still don't know what he really believes about God. I don't think he thinks religion is silly — he's much too intellectually complacent for that — but if I had to guess, I'd say he thinks it exists so people can make a necessary, respectable fuss on holidays in order to feel part of the clan. That religion is part of the dues paid for respectability. My mother may feel the same. I've never asked either of them about it.

When I was eight, my mother refused to take me to church any longer because I gave a ferocious pinch to the back of the neck of an old man who'd fallen asleep in the pew in front of us. I'd seen plenty of people fall asleep but this one was close enough for me to smite. I saw it that way: smiting. (I was a real brute of a child. I bloodied a dozen noses before I entered high school.) I was glad to not have to go anymore. Instead of listening to the sermons, I'd been reading the Bible — straight through to Revelation and then again — and I knew we were sitting in the kind of church that Jesus would have spit out of his mouth. Lukewarm, neither hot, nor cold. Massachusetts clapboard moribund.

I did not like church but I wanted an absolute and I wanted its demands.

I studied classics at Harvard partially because I wanted to know about the civilizations that cradled Christianity. The other part was because I was a pompous ass. Ted likes to say that I studied classics because I wanted to know where Western civilization came from, the better to conquer it through literature.

So I was studying and speaking out against every triumph of the powerful over the powerless. I led demonstrations. Against conscription, against segregation, against McCarthy. I broke my arm while trying to climb up the side of Memorial Church at a protest against the bomb. I filled the *Crimson* with screeds on what I thought a so-called Christian democracy should look like. I led a hunger strike for a few days to protest the college's hiring of a right-wing ideologue whose work was a tract against welfare. I passed out on the third day. My father threatened to stop paying the bills if, as he said, I pulled "a stunt like that again." And I did all this thinking of Christ. I did not go to church, but I kept Christ in mind as I acted. Whatever you have done unto the least of my brethren, you have done unto me. Whoever helps one of these little ones in my name, helps me.

Maria. Maria was in a class of mine when I was a junior. She was dark-haired, dark-eyed, pale — some great fire from within had consumed her and then expired, leaving her white and stark. Maria was Russian, from Brooklyn. She and I slept together quite a bit. I didn't think that I loved her but I knew I liked sleeping with her. I thought she was beautiful, and I wanted to have something beautiful. But then I got the feeling I was an amusement for her. Like Babe the Blue Ox — some big strong dumb American animal who put its blind trust in what it believed, charging and snorting all over the place, rushing toward goals it would never achieve. Her grandfather had been put to death by Stalin and she thought that to be politically engaged was the height of naiveté. She once told me that she thought I might one day be great but that I had to stop thinking God was going to have anything to do with it. She thought that my belief in God made me a child, that only a spoiled child could think God existed. This was invigorating but it also drove me mad. I had started to believe that I might love her in some way. I came to her room late at night once when I was drunk, shouting, throwing myself at her because I wanted her to respect me more than I thought she did. I wanted her to want me more than she did — I mean, I didn't want her to look at me as if I were a child, I wanted her to look at me with hunger. She tried to kick me out. I called her a whore. I woke up the next morning outside her door with blood crusted around my nostrils and over my upper lip — the remains of a bloody nose. She told me later that she'd pushed me away, and when she did my legs twisted up beneath me, which sent me crashing to the floor, which gave me the bloody nose. She told me she'd thought about calling the police but then decided that that was an overreaction. She wanted nothing more to do with me. I used to get in fights all the time in school — anyone without an older brother, I came to his defense, and this was partly a function of my being an only child and missing the chance to be heroic for a younger sibling — but this was different. I had been violent toward a woman. This made me sick. I started to feel nauseated when I thought about how bellicose, how thunderous, I'd been all my childhood — and I saw my time at Harvard as childhood. I thought I had been growing up by unleashing my strength and mind onto the world, by imposing myself and not being afraid of it, but this suddenly began to seem like a lifetime of tantrums. I'd gotten used to having too much, at having whatever I willed become real, which had made my will promiscuous. Not strong at all.

My mother had a story she would occasionally tell me whenever I refused to go to some family engagement or to dress up for these engagements, or when I rejected their offers of money or their ideas about law school. "When you were about four years old," she would say, "someone gave you a scooter for a present. And one afternoon, when you were out with your father, you kept trying to see how far you could go." At one point my father told me to come back, but I just kept rolling on. "No one can stop me," I am supposed to have said, "only God." I thought about that story many times after what happened with Maria. I started to feel that I needed to stop thinking only God could stop me. Perhaps I should try to submit myself to God, rather than try to be him.

Then, at the start of my senior year, a theologian came to dinner at a professor's house and we talked. He spoke of Maritain, who said that art was the practical virtue of the intellect (you know this), and after reading Maritain I decided that art should be my action, and that I should become a Catholic. It was as simple as that. It happened in one night.

And I wondered, I still wonder — I want to think deeply and not have it carry me off to some place where I'm useless. I mean, I carry myself off enough when I write, and I fear that, although it may make me great, it may make me useless as well. My politics might become an unintelligible mess. I saw in that theologian, in his Catholicism, a way to make a sustained and coherent statement about what I believed. And that seemed a sign — when you see what is possible, and you become less afraid. I became a Catholic that Easter.

So I was a senior, and I could have gone on to get a PhD after graduating, but I decided to become a Trappist monk instead. My parents were livid. They still imagined that I would suddenly straighten up at the end of college and decide to go to law school, which demonstrates how little they know me, or want to know me. I went to a monastery in Virginia for about two months that summer. At the monastery, the monks thought — they knew — I meant well. But there was the sense that I would not last. Near the end of the summer, the abbot said he thought he saw me, as he put it, sweating at the communion rails. He told me to go back out into the world. He did not want me using the religious life as atonement or refuge. He thought that if I persisted I would eventually be miserable. He thought I would be better off living a faith in the world, writing of God to the world from the world. In the monastery, he thought, I would try too hard; I would make a commotion. He told me that my penance would be noisy, but it would not make a joyful noise, and because my penance would not be joyful, it might distract my other brothers. He was not saying, he told me, that a religious life should be free of anguish, but that there was joy in the Psalms too, and he thought that it might be easier for me to find joy, if I could find it, in the world, in marriage, maybe, he said, and family. He thought I needed to be among people, not to renounce them. He reminded me that Maritain was not a priest.

Then, seeking a way to be prostrate before God while also in the world, I went to a Catholic Worker, the one in the East Village. And soon I got asked to leave. This involved a girl. A girl who lived there thought I liked her too much. She was bothered by the fact that I had written her a few poems. (Yes, I suppose that can look rather menacing if the one writing is well past his teenage years.) She once told me that the amount of time I spent in confession had convinced her that I saw it not as an opportunity for contrition but as a chance to perform an aria. This girl was a blonde. She wore her hair in braids. Her name was Ellen. Her soul seemed clean and well ordered, and now that I think about it, I might have gotten that impression solely from her braids, her tightly, very tightly, woven brass-gold braids. They had me thinking of the purity and severity of childhood. With those braids, and her padded pink-and-ivory face, forehead an imperiously vaulted arch, I'd turned her into a long-lost virgin companion of Saint Ursula — have you seen those Flemish busts at the Cloisters?

Now I see that I mistook her severity for true spiritual radiance, but at the time, when I was convinced I was in love with her, I told myself that perhaps the abbot had been right, and God had led me out of the monastery because he knew celibacy would be disastrous for me. Because I thought I was in love with this girl, and I was writing poems in this place, where I was also doing good, I hoped. So even after I was asked to leave, I was undaunted, because I had learned a lesson, I thought, and I had had a sign, which was that I did not need to be constrained within the bounds of a religious community, whether lay or ordered, to live a Christian life.

Then I spent the last year before the colony in New York, reading manuscripts and writing. And then I went to the colony, where I met you.

Yours,
Bernard

March 1, 1958

Bernard —

Dear God, Bernard! Such strenuous effort. I got worn out from reading about it. A Trappist monastery! I see how lazy a Christian I have been. Your letter gave me a complex. But I think you and I have a little something in common.

When I was about eight, there was a nun who was out to get me. She answered me with sarcasm when I asked questions and in general behaved as if I were an unwanted foundling strapped to her already overburdened back. Even as a kid, I knew this sister had it in for me because I asked questions. I was always polite when I asked them, but I asked them, and this drove her crazy because it meant that I was onto her small mind.

One day she started to ask a question of the class — I forget what it was — and in my eagerness to answer I spoke before she finished her sentence. "Frances," she snapped, looking straight at me, "that's enough out of you." That was the last straw. I shot up from my desk. "Sister, why are you talking this way to me?" I said.

"And what way is that?" she said, the tips of her fingers resting on the desk, standing tall, waiting in insolence for more insolence.

Apprehensive, anticipatory silence from the girls behind me. "You're being mean to me for no reason."

"But you interrupted me."

"Sister," I said, "if we say that we have not sinned, we make him a liar, and his word is not in us." It was a passage from John that had been read to us at Mass the week before. It seemed like a shotgun you could pull out to use on people when they got out of line.

I was sent to the Reverend Mother. My father had to go in and smooth it all over. He told me I could not talk back to any of my teachers until I went to college because his part-time job as the church groundskeeper — he worked at a printing press during the week — allowed me and my sister, Ann, to go to the school for free. "Those nuns aren't holier than the rest of us," my father said to me. "They've never known the love of anyone but God, if that. But they have been charitable to us, and you need to be kind to them. You'll never lose anything in being kind, Frances." I felt no kindness toward them, but I bit my tongue after that. I did it for my father, not for the nuns. I like to think Jesus has forgiven me that sin because I had only just lately arrived at the age of reason. I think if my sister, Ann, had been kicked out and gone to public school, my father wouldn't have minded so much. But he was intent on my earning a scholarship and getting for myself what he couldn't give me. He loved us both — loves us both — but he was not very good at hiding his delight in my brain. And Ann is not very good at hiding her mistrust of it. "The only way those books will keep you warm is if you burn them," she likes to say. She thinks I'm no better than those nuns after all. I often fear she may be right.

But I don't want to forget to say that it's a common mistake to confuse severity for spiritual radiance. I think many religious folk mistakenly champion the importance of being ramrod. Especially religious folk who have coagulated into a group.

Yours,
Frances

March 10, 1958

Frances —

I feel a kinship with your father: I delight in your brain as well.

If we had been schoolchildren together, you would have barely tolerated me. When you heard me talking my head off in class you would have given me the look you gave all of us at the colony whenever you heard us making plans to drive to a bar in town. A look that would have been even more formidable coming from the large blue eyes in a small girl's face.

I delight also in your continuous chide. And here I rewrite myself. Regarding what I wrote in my previous letter: No one has been able to stop me, not even God. What I mean is that not even God has been able to save me from myself. This is one thing I despair of. I plunge myself into something, seeing and hearing only my will, and I have to crash into something else to stop — Maria, the monastery, the Catholic Worker. So I don't know if I can say that I have ever heard God's voice. I wonder if it was only my own will, speaking loudly, that led me to the monastery, the Catholic Worker, even conversion. I wonder if you think we can ever hear God's voice. I suspect you would call me naive for imagining such a thing is possible.

It's good to have people around me to put their hands on my shoulders and get me moving forward again. Maria may have been trying to but I could not hear her. But I can frequently hear Ted.

Ted came to visit me at the Catholic Worker. We were sitting in the kitchen having coffee while people made dinner, and a fight broke out over how much meat to use in the soup, and he said: "I think the people here have problems. And by *people,* I mean you." I didn't, and don't, think Ted's entirely right, because he comes from a family whose coal companies bust unions, but this was right after the girl scolded me, so what he said — about me — seemed right.

Your story reminded me that I, too, love John best. There is a verse of his that presses on me: *This then is the message which we have heard of him and declare unto you; that God is light, and in him there is no darkness at all.* I can grow dark. I grow black. It is not, I think, what defines me, this blackness, but it is something that runs through me and can overtake me. The blackness is a hand that passes over my face to draw me a bath of heavy, ache-riven sleep, and if I want to come out of it I have to make a constant effort to see what is going on around me and then decide if I want to care about where to put my feet and hands. Impatient only for something to drag me off into unconsciousness. No desire even to write. I look at typewritten drafts, and the sentences slide off the paper and trail off into the distance; the sentences break up into letters, hovering like a cloud of gnats over my typewriter. This hand can also draw me a bath of drink, or send me crashing into people. I have stood on street corners fantasizing about being hit by a car — about being taken out instantly. Stood asleep on street corners summoning dreams of traffic accidents. I was once fantasizing about this on a corner somewhere in Cambridge and at that same moment, one traffic light down, two cars crashed into each other, and I fainted from the shock of hearing sounds I'd been practicing summoned — but not summoned close enough. And then came to in an emergency room hammering down rudeness on the nurses because I was still alive.

I wonder if I should have even described this to you, if I have scared you. But I imagine knowing you for a long, long time, and I have felt this blackness for a long, long time, and I don't want to hide any part of my self from you.

Yours,
Bernard

March 13, 1958

Bernard —

You don't scare me. I have not experienced feelings like that myself, but I think my mother suffered from them. I don't think I can tell you anything that can lift you out of this blackness — here is where I may have a little blackness myself, in refusing to believe that humans can bulldoze each other out of despondency by applying the force of uplifting sentiment — but please don't be afraid to write to me about it.

You're right. I probably would have given you that look had we been classmates — and yes, I was giving all of you that look at the colony, but not really you specifically, although there was that one night I saw you fingering Lorraine's necklace while you were all making plans to drive out, and I have to tell you I always thought you were too nice to Lorraine. I assumed it was because she was the only pretty thing there, and you couldn't help yourself around pretty things. I know I can judge like an Irish mother-in-law, but I don't think I was too far off. However, feel free to contest.

But back to school: I would have quoted scripture to you, too, if I thought you liked the sound of your own voice too much: *If I speak with the tongues of men, and of angels, but have not charity, I am become as sounding brass, or a tinkly cymbal.* I would have nicknamed you the Sounding Brass. And you could have called me Tiny Methuselah.

Do I think we can ever hear God's voice? Well, this goes back to what I said earlier — I think it might be dangerous to believe we hear him. I am suspicious of what we take to be signs — they may be only our own desires reflected back to us in an ostensibly fortuitous event. Simone Weil horrifies me, but I also believe a great deal of what she says is from God. Your question makes me think of something she has written: "But this presence of Christ in the host is not a symbol either, for a symbol is the combination of an abstraction and an image; it is something which human intelligence can represent to itself; it is not supernatural." Whatever we may think we hear will be corrupted, or as she would say, debased.

To ask to hear God's voice, to ask for signs — this seems to me impertinence of the highest order.

My aunts and my sister, however, would cluck their tongues at me and say that I have intellectualized myself out of one of the great pleasures of the Catholic faith: signs and wonders, and a network of saints to arrange for them. They certainly do believe God talks to us, and with a megaphone. My grandmother was big on praying for parking spots. "Help me out here, Lord," she'd say when circling for one. "What if you're dialing him and he's busy?" I used to say. She'd laugh and tell me "Oh, hush," and Ann would snip at me when we got out of the car, say that it wasn't right to talk that way. Ann has snipped at me all her life. My aunt Peggy believes in the song of Bernadette and helps raise money for people to go to Lourdes. Ann can always turn a disappointment into a sign of God's promise that something better will come along. The women in my family certainly do feel that his will will be done. My aunts all think that it's God's will that my mother died when she did. They have to. They have intimated to me and Ann that she was "unhappy." I have figured out that what they mean is that she was hospitalized for a nervous breakdown right after she married my father. I overheard them talking one day two years ago. They do not know I know this, and I am curious to see if they will ever bring it up. My father never will. And I won't — to him, at least. Who knows what he went through? I can't bear knowing, and I don't think he could bear explaining. It's none of my business. I believe that he loved us as fiercely as he did as a way to extinguish the sorrow.

Forgive me. I didn't mean to go on that long. Bernard, I have a sneaking suspicion that one day you will get me to confess to all sorts of things without my realizing it.

But then there's prayer and discernment. Prayer is a mystery I should not approach. I'm not very good at it. I don't really do it unless I have it written out for me. Anything I came up with on my own would sound like my asking for a pony for Christmas.

Speaking of prayer, here's something about Simone Weil that kills me. She says that it's sort of humorous, the line "Our father, who art in heaven." To think that we, so far from him, really could knock and receive him, when the distance is so great. I'm the last person to want to describe God as a constantly available warm lap, but this strikes me as self-abasement taken to an absurd degree. And then she writes: "Each time that we say 'Thy will be done' we should have in mind all possible misfortunes added together." But her line is what seems like a joke to me — to say that God's love always makes Jobs out of us. It's like something Mencken or Twain would put in the mouth of a cynical reverend. I do believe with her that suffering is one way to hear God, or to know God. Or maybe we hear God when, per John, we sense that we are making him out to be a liar and his word is not in us. When we are aware of the distance between God and ourselves, because we are sinning, then we hear him — he emerges when we are ashamed of our nakedness, so to speak.

Then there are times that I think her theology might have sprung fully formed from her migraines.

28

Bernard, I do not want you to feel black. My prayers may be faulty, but know that whenever I pray I will be praying for your sky to rarely look ominous.

Yours,
Frances

March 31, 1958

Frances —

I'm so very sorry about your mother. I say all sorts of terrible things about mine, but if she died I think it would be as if there were, finally, no God. I am very glad, though, that you were as loved as you were.

Thinking about calling you Tiny Methuselah makes me considerably less black. Thinking about you in general makes me considerably less black.

I like to think of you praying such a lovely prayer. Thank you.

No, no, I do like pretty things. It's the thorn in my flesh, as Paul would say. Lorraine wanted to be looked at, and I liked looking at her, in the way you can like looking at a view — you don't need the view, but it's nice that it's there and you've come upon it, so it wasn't as if I were robbing her of her virtue just by looking at her. Looking at someone who wants to be looked at — you know that's not real sin, Frances, and you shouldn't be jealous.

I have read Weil, and I do think she is right, mostly, as you say. She is right for this, too: "Men owe us what we imagine they will give us. We must forgive them this debt. To accept the fact that they are other than the creatures of our imagination is to imitate the renunciation of God. I am also other than what I imagine myself to be. To know this is forgiveness."

When I read this, I wince. Whenever I have imagined anyone to be other than what he or she is, whenever I have imagined myself to be other than what I am — here is where I have run into the most trouble in my life. That is when, as you say, I am ashamed of my nakedness. But I grow blind about that nakedness so easily.

She's right, but you're right about her too! I read her and think — if the Lord's prayer is a joke, are the Psalms a joke? What is joy to her? All her ecstasies are in self-negation. She's completely neurotic about the pull of other people, people as idols. I feel that we are reading someone castigating herself for having loved too much, or having been wronged by her own faith in another. And yet how can I complain about her? Who hasn't idolized and in that idolizing come to grief? She is a seer like John. She's the voice of Jesus when he says I have come to divide houses against each other. When I complain about her severity, it's because I want my sin.

Or is that true?

Still, I think there's too much Buddhism in her for me. And too much of Augustine in me to appreciate her — to think that love, happiness, and joy aren't as intelligible, and truly evident, as suffering.

Yours,
Bernard

April 5, 1958

Bernard, I am not jealous. I believe that thought, to borrow a phrase from Sr. Weil, is a creature of your imagination. I laughed out loud when I read it. Oh, Bernard. Surely you know not every girl's worth looking at. And not every girl is a jealous girl. Surely in your net-casting you have discovered this. I wasn't jealous. I was, I repeat, being judgmental. You were two people playing at affection, it seemed, and as someone who reserves affection for only a select few, I thought this comfort on the stage was a little disturbing.

But this was before I knew you. I have to admit that at lunch that day, and for some time after, I had an idea that you might be something of a cad. I don't think you're a cad now. But perhaps there is too much of Augustine in you!

I do have great affection for Augustine, even if I don't understand his appetites and the power they had over him.

Yours,
Frances

April 17, 1958

Dear Frances —

I'm going to read that last line of your last letter to mean that you also have great affection for me. This pleases me immensely.

Unfortunately, I have been a cad. Blindness makes for caddishness. Cruelty's not the only way to be a cad. Although I have been cruel too.

I am curious — have you ever singled out someone for your affection? I've been wanting to ask this. Do not misunderstand my tone here; I ask with all the tenderness and innocence of a brother. Imagine me asking: Frances, what did you read as a child? And that is how I am asking this question.

You have made me uncharacteristically circumspect. I like that very much.

Yours,
Bernard

April 27, 1958

Dear Bernard —

There was a young man for whom I had affection at Iowa. He is now married to the woman who was my best friend at the time. That is all I will say about that.

Except to tell you that I found my dearest friend, Claire, because of this young man. I was in the ladies' room during a dance crying in a stall because the young man had chosen this particular evening to break it off, and Claire happened to be in the next stall over. I kept flushing the toilet because I didn't want anyone to hear me, because I was so ashamed of crying over him, and in public, but she heard the keening of self-pity above the tsunami of flushing and knocked on the stall. "Are you all right over there?" she said. "Can I get you some water, or an aspirin, or a drink?" I didn't answer right away and she said, "Are you crying over someone?" That made me cry even harder, and Claire came out of her stall, washed her hands, and waited for me. "I don't want to tell you how many times I've cried in the ladies' room at dances," she said through the door. "It's revolting, I know. You hate yourself for it." I liked that she used the word *hate*. I came out of the stall and saw a tall blonde in an emerald-green shantung shift, her hair swept up on top of her head. She looked at me and said: "What a fetching dress!" I told her I'd made it myself. Now it's two years later and I don't know what I'd do without her. That was the first and last school dance I ever attended, by the way. I'd rather go to a funeral.

Now, tell me what you read as a child.

Yours,
Frances

May 7, 1958

Dearest Frances —

I've done some shabby things, but I've never thrown a girl over for her friend. I pray I never do. But it sounds like you won, in the end, if such a thing as Claire transpired shortly after.

Permit me to lecture for a moment: Uncle Bernard says that unless you, like Kierkegaard, are desiring and capable of basing a

32

whole system of philosophy around this rejection, you should fall in love again. And again and again, if you have to. It is one of life's greatest pleasures.

I can hear your eyes rolling all the way up here in Boston. Your blue, blue eyes.

As commanded: here is what I read as a child, ranked in order of moral and aesthetic influence.

The Bible. All the way through at seven years old and then repeatedly, daily, as of noon today, at breakfast. Psalm 51. King James Version.

Paradise Lost. At eleven years of age. My affinity for the devil was almost as terrifying to me as the idea of him.

The Iliad and *The Odyssey.* Eight. *With these words he led the way and the others followed after with a cry that rent the air, while the host shouted behind them.*

Bulfinch's Mythology. Eight.

Hamlet, at twelve.

Dickens's *A Child's History of England.* At seven. I began by imagining myself as Alfred, but by the end worshiped Cromwell, because he was a Puritan, too, and I drafted the neighborhood boys into a New Model Army. There was a mutiny soon after, I don't think I need to tell you, that sent me indoors for the rest of the summer reading—

Treasure Island.

Brothers Grimm, Hans Christian Andersen. Read them over and over when I was six, which is when I decided that I wanted to marry a mermaid. I had a habit of swimming too far out to find them and would have to be dragged bodily out of the Atlantic by my father. After one of these episodes, while I shivered on the sand wrapped in a tartan blanket, I heard my grandmother, my mother's mother, who sat immobilized beneath a parasol like an iceberg dressed in black, more tartan blankets covering the diabetic gangrenous foot that I was always told to keep out of the way of, say: "The only way you're going to get that boy to behave is by running him over with a car. Pity you can't." And then she winked at me. I have often thought that my father was frightened by what he imagined was the beginning of the disease of lovesickness — the same disease that had had him panting after my mother, who by this point in their marriage had turned like milk; now she was a materialistic withholding scold. But I more than made up for whatever softness he feared by a period of prepubescent pugilism, a reign of terror in which I pulped anyone who wouldn't let me take charge or have my way. This subsided, mostly, in high school, though I did, my first year at Harvard, throw a punch at Ted. I missed. He, in response, knocked me out. This is why I conscripted him into a friendship. We cannot for the life of us remember why I threw a punch at him. Ted likes to say it was because we showed up to the bar wearing the same dress.

When I ask my freshmen what they have read, they all stare at me for a moment, and then talk about television and comic books. Could a gap of eight or so years really make that much difference? I suppose you and I could have been listening to cereal-sponsored serials on the radio, but we didn't — or did you? I can tell you, however, that *Superman* is actually quite an amazing read, should you find yourself at a drugstore lunch counter with all the day's papers sold out.

Love (may I?),
Bernard

May 8, 1958

Dear Frances —

I wrote and mailed, forgetting that I'd wanted to ask the following.

Would you like to contribute to the *Charles Review*? I can't pay you, but I can offer you publication in an esteemed journal, your words jostling alongside those of Pulitzer winners and expatriate literary lions. I won't put you near the Iowan chaff.

Yours,
Bernard

May 16, 1958

Dear Uncle Bernard —

Your niece Frances — a four-eyed, French-plaited platypus awaiting the evaporation of her baby fat — thanks you very much for the romantic advice. But I've never been one to spend time thinking about why men and women take to each other, or why they don't. I think it can turn a lady neurotic, a term I despise but also am loath to have turned in my direction.

I think I read more like your students! I had a period where I was reading lots of comic books — one of my uncles drove a truck for a magazine distributor and always brought home tons of whatever didn't sell. So I agree — *Superman* is really quite an amazing read. As an excuse for this, I'm going to say that in my child's mind, comic books were as potboiling and morally clear as Bible stories, and that was why I ate them up. I read a lot of Nancy Drew too, even though I knew it was the same story over and over again. When I'd read all of them and back again, my aunts piled a lot of Judy Bolton on me, thinking I'd love that too. Not the same. I read them all, though, in a summer, hoovering like they were Cracker Jack. Fell asleep reading them on the beach down the shore and got sunburned. And I didn't really even like them. Sometimes I wonder if the automatic way I consumed them, one after the other, thinking of nothing but getting to the next one but without real appreciation for the taste, means I have it in me to be an alcoholic. Then I think that reading — something, anything — was maybe a way to hide in a family where I was always required to be in plain sight. Nobody approved of being antisocial. Anyway. I didn't read *Treasure Island,* but I did read *The Swiss Family Robinson. Robinson Crusoe* too. I really did love *Little Women,* although I could not stand that the girls called their mother something so sissy as Marmee, and you will not be surprised to hear that I identified with Jo and pictured Ann whenever Amy popped up. *Little Women* was one of several books my mother had owned and that my aunts gave me the Christmas I was eight; the others were *Heidi, Wuthering Heights,* and *Jane Eyre.* The next Christmas, my father gave me the books he'd read in childhood — and that was how I read nearly all of Dickens. I am looking at these old books on my shelf as I write to you. Their leather is as dark as dirt now, and the tops of the spines are fraying. If this place burned down they would be the first thing I grabbed.

I did not read *Paradise Lost* until about a year ago, I'm afraid. (I have to say, I agree with you about Satan being the draw. Adam and Eve: Who cares?) Can you find it within yourself to keep up a correspondence with this northeastern hillbilly? Uncle Bernard, maybe you should send me a box full of Greek tragedy — perhaps this is what I really need, more than advice for the lovelorn. Or perhaps Greek tragedy *is* advice for the lovelorn! You tell me.

As to your second letter: I would love to be published in the *Charles Review.* I'm enclosing a chapter from the novel. If this offends, no offense taken. Will I also receive a handsome muffler with the *Charles Review* stitched into it? I look best in green and gray.

Yours,
Frances

May 28, 1958

Dear Frances —

Am so pleased that you will contribute. I warn you, I will edit. Since the last time you wrote, I've grown a little dark. Ted has proposed to, and been accepted by, this woman who will, very shortly after they marry, certainly seduce him into going to law school. Which will not be difficult, because Ted's novel has been rejected by several houses, and he doesn't have the confidence to keep going. He should keep going, but I think he will escape from this catastrophe — what he feels to be a catastrophe, because he'd told himself that if he couldn't publish this book, he would give up on writing — into domesticity. He was waiting to be saved into writing but now has to ask this woman to save him into the next thing, which will be a comfortable haute bourgeois existence, with children, just like the one his parents led. Ted doesn't need much, but he does need to look extremely capable, and he knows he could lawyer and he knows he could make money, because his family has been making money for generations. (Ted, against my vociferous rumblings, ran a lucrative poker game out of our rooms at Harvard. I don't mind gambling on my own physical strength, or talent, or attractiveness, but there's something about gambling away money that makes me queasy. Must be the Puritan in me.) I haven't said anything to him about this woman. But I think he knows what I think, and this is making the apartment strangely, portentously quiet.

Kay is the daughter of a congressman from Mississippi. I almost wrote *clergyman,* and I think that there is some provincial parsimony dripping off her aquiline nose. She's too beautiful to be a harridan, but she has the soul of one. One weekend when she came to visit and Ted and I ran out for more liquor, she emptied all of our ashtrays on the floor, sat waiting at the dining room table for us to come back, and said: "I'll clean this all up but I wanted you two to understand how disgusting it is to live as you do, especially from a lady's standpoint." "I'll clean it up, *lady,*" he said, with an emphasis on that last word, and she and I stared each other down while Ted went to get the broom. I can see why Ted's in love with her. She possesses the tenderness of a portrait of Dora Maar, and the forceful will to conquer realities that has been exhibited by all the southern women I have met. She looks like the daughter of a sixteenth-century Spanish innkeeper and views her life's journey as akin to Sherman's march to the sea. She is beautiful. I should despise Ted, because it's the kind of marriage you'd make if you needed money or wanted to get into politics, and Ted sure as hell doesn't need money and thinks politics is a game utopians follow because baseball bores them. (As I write, I hear you wondering, as I sometimes wonder: Why am I friends with Ted? Well, he's one of the smartest people I know, and when I met him I felt that our blood boiled at the same temperature, even though it might not be set to boil by the same writers, the same injustices, or the same women. It is one of those relationships in which a semi-inexplicable current of respect for the other's intensity and strength is responsible for the bond.) So I don't despise Ted, even though I think what he is doing is setting himself up to follow the family line out of a lack of courage. The old story, and still an enraging story. No, I despise her.

Frances, tell me if I am in the wrong here. I don't trust any of the women I know in Boston to tell me the truth.

Love,
Bernard

June 4, 1958

Dear Bernard —

I'm very sorry to hear about Ted. I'm going to take Shakespeare a little out of context: "Go to, I'll no more on 't; it hath made me mad. I say, we will have no more marriages."

The women on my mother's side of the family, my three aunts and my grandmother, they all married well enough and out of the immigrant melodrama of innumerable babies and strife, but growing up I saw how they seemed to do nothing but cook, clean, scold, and sew. It appeared that mothering was being maid and confessor to three to seven people. Or more, if you took your Catholicism seriously. Which, as I have already established, my aunts did. They were always giving safe harbor to the kids in the neighborhood who did live in the strife — inviting them for dinners, cutting their hair, giving them my cousins' castoffs. My aunts ran an ad hoc mission out of their homes. Ann, who would marry a stray dog if she could, has a great deal of them in her. This is why I won't marry. I am not built for self-abnegation. If I'm built for anything, it's writing. I can't even teach! I had to, when I was at Iowa, but I was not very good at hiding my displeasure at mental sleepiness and mediocrity. And if anyone gets my self-abnegation, it needs to be the Lord. He's been waiting a very long time for it. He'll be pleasantly surprised one of these days if it ever shows up.

I approve wholeheartedly of the marriage of Claire and Bill — Claire is a reporter and Bill teaches Latin at an expensive Catholic boys' school, and I don't think I'll ever see two people as in love with each other as they are. It makes me think that a marriage of true minds — to again quote S. — is in many ways just dumb luck. Two of my childhood friends have married men I think are complete dullards. One of them I might even describe as a lout. This husband, drunk at their Christmas party, said that he'd always wondered if I was a lesbian but that I must not be because a lesbian couldn't possibly look that good in black velvet. I told him that he didn't know much about lesbians then. But the wives do not seem to mind the way I mind. They do not see their husbands as extensions of their personalities; they see them as means to motherhood and material comfort. They seem happy with their children, happy with their dresses and their homes. They seem happy and oblivious. Sometimes I think they have happened upon a spiritual discipline I might do well to adopt. When I do not think they're fools.

I wonder if Ted isn't just after his own version of this happiness? I know that thinking of it this way is no consolation. I have never been good at thinking myself out of disappointment, so take this for what it's worth. Some people don't need more than what's in front of them. Mostly I feel just fine about not having this talent but sometimes (see above) — well, I'll just say "but sometimes," and leave it at that. I don't know Ted, but if he can talk back to this lady, I think he knows what he's about.

I'm going to shut up now. You're not in the wrong.

Yours,
Frances

June 10, 1958

Dear Frances —

Your letter did help. I know that this is probably just a boy's recalcitrance to accept the fact that romance takes different shapes among us. What makes Ted feel like he's alive is not what makes me feel alive, and it may be that Ted doesn't need to be as alive as I do, and I have to accept that. When a friend stops reflecting you back to yourself in a way that keeps your vanity buffed and shined — that's all this is, I suppose. There is something in my bones that senses eventual divorce, however.

All right, all right, enough, enough. I will keep in mind what Frances the Spiritual Director has suggested.

Love to you —
Bernard

June 26, 1958

Bernard —

I got a job in New York. Did you know I can type like a demon? Well, I can, and this talent has led me to be hired as Alfred Sullivan's secretary at Sullivan and Shields. Jeanette, a friend of mine from Iowa who lives in New York mingling among the literary, has been keeping her ear to the ground for me and when she heard of this she thought I would be perfect for it. Alfred Sullivan, as you know, is seventy-nine and almost senile but still vain about his father's name, and thus he needs to be placated so he'll keep paying everyone. Alfred Sullivan needs a secretary. Or the illusion of a secretary, and here's where I come in. The old one died. She was sixty-seven. She'd been with him for thirty years. She might even have been his mistress, but no one's saying. And if he dies after a year, at least I will have gotten to New York. Her name was Frances too. I believe Mr. Sullivan is a superstitious, sentimental old Irish fool.

Which I am very grateful for, because his patronage is making it possible for me to stay at the Barbizon. Do you know this place? Actresses, writers, models, secretaries, convented away from menfolk so they can play at being career girls without being molested before they get married — when they'll be molested legally. Another nunnery. But I get my own room, and meals are provided, and it's clean and cheap. Mr. Sullivan wrote me a letter of reference, and he got another big shot at the house to write one for me too. I think, after nearly a year of waitressing and keeping house for my father and Ann, I will allow myself to enjoy a certain amount of paternalism.

This job has come at the right time. When I begin to be short with my father at the dinner table, I know things have gone sour.

I thought you might like to know this news. I hope you're feeling better.

Yours,
Frances

July 2, 1958

Dear Frances —

I laughed out loud at your letter. I congratulate you. If a writer has to have a job, serving as handmaiden to the obsolete is the best kind to have. This nunnery, however, sounds ridiculous. Make me proud and get kicked out of there, won't you?

And I've read your chapter. It's fantastic. I have one thought: the ending is too abrupt. I think the problem is that you, the author, know what's coming next in the book and can rest easy in that knowledge, but maybe there's a way that you can adjust for those who don't have that privilege. No, I have a second thought: I am hungry for Sister to say one thing that gives evidence of her theology — that she has a theology.

I really do think it's wonderful. You make me ashamed of all my words.

Yours,
Bernard

July 9, 1958

Dear Bernard —

I can't tell you how glad I am that you liked what I sent you. But I don't want to change a thing. If there is lingering discomfort at the end, all the better.

I write you from my shoebox in the Barbizon. I have a tiny window. It looks out onto Sixty-Third Street, and since I am up high, the sunsets have been lovely evening companions. This place is very clean, which I require. But why are women so awful? Everyone's perfectly nice — which is the problem. At dinner, the only thing they can think to ask me about, after my job, is whether I'm going with anyone. When I answer no, cheerfully, and keep eating, you can feel the pity and suspicion tiptoeing around in their silence. Since they can't make their pity or suspicion public, they have to be encouraging: "Oh, you'll find someone, I'm sure. It's a big city!" It's like eating dinner with my sister, only multiplied by eight to ten. Though my sister knows how to make a joke. These girls have some money — they're daughters of doctors and lawyers and bankers — and I think money eliminates the need for the catharsis of humor. Kierkegaard says that comedy transpires in the gap between the eternal and the temporal, and I think that these girls, because they have not known the disappointment of being caught between what one hopes for and what one actually receives, can't make jokes. But you know more rich people than I do, so correct me if I'm wrong.

The job is a joke.

I can't invite you up to my chamber, but I could have you to dinner if you come to visit. Do you like instant mashed potatoes? I do. They are on offer every night.

Yours,
Frances

July 16, 1958

Dear Frances —

I'm so glad you're happy. That place sounds as ridiculous as I imagined. I send you my pity, made public. But women are awful for the same reason men are awful: limited scope. And the rich can too make jokes. About their help, in whom they are constantly disappointed.

I see your point about the ending. I suppose I ask for more clarity in prose than I ask for in poetry. That is chauvinistic of me. You're lucky I like you. Otherwise I would stare you down. As I have had to stare down even the expatriate literary lion, over a line of Latin he had incorrectly translated.

I would like to come and see you very much. There are a number of people I could stay with. I don't have much to do this summer, seeing as how I've been given the fall semester off to start this new book.

I do sometimes wish we were in the same city. I do often wish we were in the same city.

Where are you going to church?

Yours,
Bernard

July 27, 1958

Bernard —

I'm going to church at Our Lady of Peace, which is on Sixty-Second Street. There's very little to recommend it other than it's convenient. The organist pounds away like she's at a Yankees game, which amuses me. The last time I went I saw the priest, making his way back down the aisle at the end of the Mass, give a little start and then purse his lips when the force of the first bars of the benediction clapped him from behind. I enjoyed that little hiccup of fallibility. But I don't think I need anything from the other people around me. I'm there for the liturgy and the host. I don't even need the homily. Like you as a child in your Congregational church.

I went to an honest-to-goodness literary cocktail party the other night, courtesy of my employer. Despite the fact that it brought back the feeling I had at the colony of being a teetotaling toddler among the lotus-eaters, I enjoyed myself. I had a substantive conversation with another secretary at the company about what we'd been reading lately. But my favorite part of the evening? Overhearing conversations about (a) a writer whose fiancée left him for the actor hired to play him in the movie version of his autobiographical novel; (b) a writer whose publisher flew her out to Los Angeles and put her up in the Ambassador Hotel to get her away from a jazz musician who was making it impossible for her to finish her second novel; and (c) the husband half of a pair of married writers, less successful and less prolific than his wife, who apparently confessed to his editor that he'd thrown out her diaphragm and gotten her drunk one night in an attempt to get her pregnant and out of the limelight for a couple of years.

Do you know that I could not catch any of the names of these people? Drat. Was being polite and trying to look interested when spoken to. Somehow I'd gotten the impression — this must have come from Iowa, where everyone paired up out of boredom and was mostly too frozen to fire up scandal — that the modern way is for writers in love to cheer each other on from their matching Scandinavian desks. But this is not the case, at least in New York. Those coolly modern Scandinavian desks do not hide the fact that things are still very barbarous between men and women.

To my point: I know you remember Jim Schultz, the *Esquire* editor who told that story at dinner one night at the colony about having his publisher expense the whorehouses Jim visited while reporting in Vietnam. Well, he came up to me at the bar when I was getting another drink and said, "Is this Frances Reardon?" "Yes," I said. "You look a shade less impregnable than last summer," he said, tapping my collarbone (I had on a boat-necked dress — forgive me if you don't know what that is; for a moment I forgot that I was writing to you and not Claire). "You look a shade more sober," I said. He laughed. It was true: hair less greasy, suit less creased. "You know my nickname for you was Fanny Price," he said. "If that's an overture," I said, "I feel compelled to inform you that the door is padlocked." He raised his glass to me and then I pointedly ignored him while I waited for my drink. I have nothing to add to that anecdote, only that it is offered up in the spirit of having suffered through the same people during a summer.

I should also tell you that I sold my book! To Scribner's. The girl who bought it seems a little young, but my agent assured me that she is, as they say, Going Places.

Why don't you come to visit next month? I would be so very

pleased to celebrate a little with you and thank you for your kindness toward my prose.

Yours,
Frances

August 2, 1958

Dear Frances —

Your book! I wish you could have seen the smile that broke across my face when I opened your letter and read the news. I'm smiling now to think of it. I hope you had your agent make them pay you what it's worth, and then some. But I'll pry the exact amount out of you when I see you.

Your description of this evening made me pant to be in New York with you, going to parties. I have to say that I'm a little surprised you took as much enjoyment as you did in that parade of envy, malice, and ambition. I suppose I imagined you would have only disparagement for those sins, that you'd leave the rejoicing in the horrors and wonders of that parade to me! You know, I think I heard that story about the diaphragm too. But I can't remember who the perpetrator was. As you said: Drat. So let me come and visit you — I would love to come and visit you — so we could go to one of these parties together and pretend to listen to each other while we eavesdrop on everyone else's conversations. You know I know where the bleeding will be heaviest.

I will admit that I heard Jim Schultz call you Fanny Price several times. Compared with what he called Lorraine, Fanny Price was downright chivalrous.

New York must have hard-boiled your heart in a cauldron of urbane indifference if Jim Schultz now touches your collarbone and you don't turn him into scrapple. I am somewhat shocked. (A former student has recently alerted me to the existence of scrapple and told me that it is beloved in your native city, which is his city too. Frances, I have to say that scrapple now makes me understand why you referred to yourself as a northeastern hillbilly. Speaking of barbarous.)

What about the weekend of the twenty-second?

Yours,
Bernard

August 25, 1958

Frances —

Thank you for letting me visit. Here is a postcard I bought at the Cloisters for you. This is Clare of Assisi as a girl receiving a palm on Palm Sunday from her bishop. They say that after this moment she disappeared from the world and gave herself over to Saint Francis and his men.

Please do not ever disappear from me.

Love,
Bernard

August 26, 1958

Ted —

Here are the books that you asked for. *Painting as a Pastime*? Your love of Churchill knows no bounds. According to this curio, he and I agree on what the soul of an artist requires: "The first quality that is needed is Audacity." You're reading like a plutocrat these days, Ted — heavy on the military history and light on novels. Is Kay that distracted by decorating your place that you need this entertainment? Although I suppose we'll now have sheets. But did we need sheets?

While I'm writing I'll tell you: that visit with Frances Reardon was quite wonderful. I took her all over the city — she hadn't dug into it yet, so we did it together. You have posited that she may have, as you like to say, *a thing* for me, but I don't think she does, and I am fairly sure I don't have one for her. I kept looking at her from different angles and examining my response. Various types of affection flared up in her presence, but not romance. I looked at her face while eating dinner at the Barbizon (that aqueduct built to conduct the flow of girls from Westchester straight into Connecticut while keeping them far above the catacombs full of dead dreams), her pretty milkmaid face flowering among all the pretty, iridescent silk-stockinged girls. And I did not find myself thinking her more beautiful than these, who were clearly nothing more than fish bred to stock the pond.

Then I watched her kneel and cross herself at Mass and she was so intent and yet unselfconscious in her movements it was as if I were watching a doe settle itself down in a green hush. Standing next to her in the pew, I felt that God truly lived within her. I didn't want to seduce her. I just wanted to settle down by her side and drink at this stream with her.

And then I sang the Agnus Dei too loudly for her tastes, and she shushed me with a shush worthy of the gargoyles at the Bodleian. At lunch afterward I must have asked her one too many questions about Etienne Gilson and she put down her knife and fork in exasperation and said, "Bernard, God is not proctoring an exam!"

She is a girl, but she is also an old man, and I see that there is intractability in her heart that may never be shattered. Perhaps that is because she grew up among women who love harder than they think, and she has strengthened her innate intractability in order to keep tunneling toward a place where she could write undisturbed by the demands of conventional femininity. So she may always think harder than she loves.

I make her smile — in spite of herself, I can tell. This appeals to the part of me that needs a conquest. That is romance enough, I think, in this particular situation. And she is wise. She might have picked that up from the women who raised her, though she might not admit it. I have not met many women who seem wise. I have met women who are shrewd, but that is a different story.

Maybe you'll meet her soon. I think you'd like her, very much. Maybe we could kidnap her and bring her to Maine and have her cook for us and tease us into submission.

Yours,
Bernard

August 26, 1958

Dear Claire —

Thank you for your letter. I wish you lived here. Or I lived there. Well, no. I don't think Chicago is for me. Those people are too damn nice! How do you stand it?

Bernard Eliot came to visit this past weekend. I think I can call him a friend. We could not stop talking. Talking to him was like talking to you — only I don't roll my eyes out of sheer exhaustion when I talk to you. So we talked. We spent five hours in a bar talking, two nights in a row. We talked. We talked, and walked. He thinks walking is "a purification," and so we walked all the way around the city, setting out from Sixty-Third and Lexington, going down the East Side, curving around the tip of the island, then all the way back up to the West Side and through Central Park and home. He lived here a few years ago and so I did enjoy seeing the city from all different angles, and being shown these angles by someone who knew the ones that made the city look its best. Though I whined a little — you know me, I love to walk, but sometimes my slothful nature makes me want to sit down somewhere and then lie down on the floor with a box of crackers within reach. When I'm done, I'm done. Especially in August. So when I whined too loudly once he put us in a cab and took me for oysters at the Oyster Bar and insisted on buying a bottle of champagne — at the counter, where he told me what he thought I ought to look for in a husband. According to Bernard, and he's thought a lot about this, I need to marry someone with money, which is not something he believes in usually, but he thinks I have the constitution for it, and the world, he said, needs my books. He says this, of course, having read one chapter of my first and only one. And after he's heard me say several times that I do not want to marry. If this had come from someone else I would have been offended, but here it amused, because Bernard loves to pontificate and regrets not having had siblings he could pontificate to. His students aren't enough. Right after he made this pronouncement he gave me a look like a taxidermist trying to decide where to start skinning and said, "I can see exactly how you would have looked in pigtails." Which means there is no enchantment afoot.

So. We went to the Cloisters. We went to Mass. (He was too boisterous a singer during the Agnus Dei and I elbowed him and reflexively whispered a shush, though I was touched because he really does seem grateful, even desperate, for God's mercy, and he just elbowed me back and kept singing.) He came to dinner two nights at the hen-house, and the girls ate him up, he was so solicitous of their aspirations, romantic and otherwise. Now, where had they gone to school? Did the young man they were dating seem serious? People are oxygen to him. It's the part of him that can stand up in front of a classroom and teach. Whereas I think being around all those kids is going to give me some sort of disease of the mind — some degenerative disease contracted from contact with their undercooked brains. He told me later, half jokingly, that he'd chatted with the girls because he wanted to thaw me out in front of them. It was hilarious. Also a little maddening. I found myself jealous of those girls! Those sorority girls! Which makes no sense. Or maybe it was that I was jealous of his ability to charm and be gracious and make it seem effortless, make it seem an extension of his intelligence. While I tend to silently judge, or make an untimely crack.

Have you seen his picture somewhere in your reading? If not: big head, long straight nose rubbery at the tip, wide forehead, large mouth, finished off by open American eyes and a mild shock of brown hair. The bigness of his head, the calm of it, filled with what it is filled with, brings to mind a marble bust that might be trying to get itself on a pedestal.

But his mind and his heart seem free of cruelty — as he talked, I saw them as two gears connected by the same belt, a belt running at top speed, frequently hiccupping and flapping at the speed and the strain before correcting itself and grinding on.

That is Bernard.

My love to Bill.

Love,
Frances

September 1, 1958

Frances —

For the month of October I am going to live on Michael Lynch's farm in West Virginia. I think you must know Michael from Iowa; he taught poetry there a few years ago. The idea is that I am going to pray and do manual labor. I've been feeling too cosmopolitan and scattered on the wind. A novelist, a girl from Kenyon, might show up too. Michael's wife, Eliza, is also a poet, and they have a young daughter named Karen. Here's my address:

Route 32, Box 2
Ravenswood, WV 26164

I hope New York is not killing you in this heat. I would ask you to come to the farm but I think I know what your answer would be.

Yours,
Bernard

September 8, 1958

Mr. Hair Shirt —

Since you know what my answer will be, I will not be reticent in letting you know what I think of Michael Lynch and his wife. He had a small crowd of acolytes that floated with him everywhere. Everyone thought that because I was Catholic and not an eighty-year-old Italian woman, I would love him too, but this was not the case. Michael and Eliza (she taught undergraduate poetry classes and taught piano too; I know you know all this, but did you know her real name is *Eileen*?) had faces that seemed cold with self-regard and I think what they imagined to be beatitude from their constant engagement with the upper regions of Catholic thought. Ugh. I read who they read, but I didn't wear what they wore. Their trying so hard to look the part of conscientious objectors made me suspicious of their purity. Pardon me — I *didn't* read exactly what they read. Dostoevsky was another Evangelist to them, the Grand Inquisitor chapter in *Bros. Karamazov* being the Sermon on the Mount. This gave me an antipathy for D. that I have just recently overcome. Eliza once came up to me after Mass and asked if I wanted to join them in praying the rosary on Sunday evenings. I demurred. When you grow up with women who pray the rosary as regularly as they do the laundry, with women to whom the laundry was a form of the rosary, it cannot be a project to reclaim it for your fancy piety. I hear that on his farm you live in sheds with the cows and piss out your window as if you were a medieval peasant.

That said, I hope you enjoy your time there. You have been busy this year, and you do deserve some rest. If you figure out a way to pray without ceasing — by which I mean without starting to wonder what you can fix for dinner — write me.

Yours,
Frances

September 16, 1958

Frances, you crank. I'll pray for your soul while I'm there. On a rosary.

Affectionately,
Mr. Hair Shirt

October 6, 1958

Bernard —

I hope your writing is going well.

I hope you do not mind me interrupting your solitude with a letter, but I turned my novel in today and wanted to tell someone who would understand that particular achievement. I am thoroughly sick of it, but I'm not sure that the people who now have it will be able to do anything to make it better. Now that the initial surprise and excitement of having a book contract have worn off, fear of the ineptness of my new editor has set in. She has recently used the word *irregardless* in a letter to my agent.

The henhouse has turned gothic. Some of the sorority girls are now bitter. "You'll do anything for a steak," I heard one of them say last week at dinner, "but then that's not all they want you to eat, the steak." So there is the suggestion that they are now choking the men down along with the steak; that both delicacies, steak and sex, have become repulsive. Then there is Regina. She is studying to be an actress and is working as a secretary. She's from Brooklyn. She has three sweaters and three skirts, she told me, which she bought to combine in six different ways. And a good black wool dress, she said, for when she has to go somewhere nice. She offered to loan me the dress once when I mentioned I had to go to a dinner for work, but I'm not keen on treating my closet like a lending library, so I said that I would prefer not to wear something that had a Dewey decimal number sewn into it. She did not laugh. It seems that several girls have gone in on that dress, but Regina paid the most, so it hangs in her closet. One night at dinner she leaned over to me and said: "Do you see that girl?" It was a girl across the room; she was talking and eating, nothing out of the ordinary. "She got in trouble," Regina said, "for using too many condiments at dinner." Then she says: "That girl and I moved here at the same time. We used to eat together, but she found those girls" — I looked at those girls, and they did seem a little more shampooed than Regina, who is bohemian manqué, like Marjorie Morningstar, only Italian, Catholic, and with an acoustic guitar — "and then that was the end of that." Regina kept looking at the girls. I kept eating. "You see the girls here turn," she said. "You see them fall prey to New York. Their hair is different, the clothes get showier, they're talking all high class where they used to talk regular, and suddenly they're not sitting with you at dinner. They're going out with men." Abruptly Regina went sour: "You just see them turn." I decided not to sit with Regina anymore, and now I have the uneasy feeling that she is going to find some other girl to turn to, then locate me in the dining room, point me out, and tell this new girl that I hoard dinner rolls and silverware. Or she may come after me with one of the dull dinner knives, scratched out of its luster by endless runs in the dishwasher, and serrate me to death in my sleep.

Then there is a woman reading her way to Christian Scientism. Her name is Sarah. From Ohio. She is overweight. I've gone to visit her room and seen a few family photographs, so I know she was once slender. You can see how she might have been a pretty chorus-girl type — sweetheart face, big eyes, blond Veronica Lake waves, rosebud lips. Her eyes are the eyes of a girl who knows she believes lies but can't do anything other than believe them. She moved in ten years ago — she wanted to sing in musicals — and she has never left. She never did really sing onstage — "Now I never will, I guess," she says, referring to her weight — but she helps run the kitchen in return for room and board. If anyone is hoarding dinner rolls, it's Sarah. She says she thanks the Lord for making this room available to her. She says she feels now that the Lord meant for her to sit quietly and figure out his mysteries through her reading, and she wouldn't exchange that opportunity for anything. Her room is full of books by people who have radio hours. It's the gospel according to Joseph Smith, Mary Baker Eddy, and Aimee Semple McPherson — American dynamism gilded into a platform for individual redemption. It's religion as detergent. I thank God I was born Catholic. At least our fairy tales involve eyes being put out and women being stretched out on racks — suggesting there is no evasion of pain and suffering. That there is no redemption without suffering, and that suffering is sometimes the point.

Where was I? Forgive me. Sarah haunts me. I think I see Ann in her. Ann isn't in the sorority girls; I was mistaken. Ann is in Sarah. They have the same eyes. Right before I left home, Ann and I had a fight. Did I tell you about this when you came? Earlier last year, my sister met a man at a dance. He was, she said, a men's-clothing buyer for Wanamaker's, and after that dance they spent a few evenings together. She fell for him. He was an Italian, handsome and traveled, and of course he dressed very, very well. He came for dinner. He was not overly ingratiating. He had manners. He asked my father about his job. He asked me what Iowa was like — he had family out there farming and couldn't imagine what it would be like to live in a place like that. But I watched him with Ann and there was an air of the waiting room about him — I got the sense that she was not a specific person to him, just someone pretty he had started chatting with while waiting to be called in for his annual. As someone who often cannot bear to be around even those people she loves, I will never understand this kind of personality — the just-dropping-by-out-of-boredom. I didn't think it was manners that kept him from looking at her with desire or with the kind of adoration that is subdued because it is in public but still obvious nevertheless. I don't know anything about romance, but I have my ideas about how people should show that they prefer each other over the vast horde. My father thought he seemed like enough of a gentleman, and to that I said yes, enough to come into a middle-class house and share a meal with strangers, but not so much that he's going to carry Ann out of here on some steed the way she wants. My father said nothing, and for a moment I regretted saying what I'd said. My father reveres romance — he thinks he and my mother had a great one — and he wants that for Ann the way he wants success for me. The problem is that Ann suspects she's beautiful but doesn't truly know it. If she did, she could be dumb and scheming like Undine Spragg and we wouldn't worry about her.

Some weeks later, this gentleman got a job in Baltimore. She wrote him. After a few letters, though, he stopped writing back. But she kept it up. She wrote a letter a month for six months. When I saw her on the sixth letter — yes, I kept count — I couldn't take it anymore. "Stop it!" I said to Ann as she sat in the kitchen writing another one. "Ann, he is never going to write back! If he's not dead, you are dead to him!"

She stood up. She looked at me in a way I had never seen her look at me — as if I were dead to her. Then she walked out to the living room, took her coat, and went for a walk. We didn't talk for a week after that.

The faith that sent Ann to her pen is the same faith that had her lighting candles for me and my book.

And I haven't even told you about the girl I saw putting paraffin on her teeth in the bathroom one Saturday night. I asked her what she was doing — this seemed like something out of a courtesan's toilette circa Versailles — and she said it covered the discoloration and crookedness of her teeth. Or the old lady who's been here for twenty years, who wears a tiny, violet-colored, violet-sprigged hat with a veil to dinner and an inordinate amount of face powder — you can see the face powder on her smart little jackets — and reportedly has papered every inch of her room with pages from movie magazines.

I think I need to move out of here. I'm five helpings of mashed potatoes away from turning into a matronly mountain that will move nowhere toward its goal.

Yours,
Frances

October 18, 1958

Frances —

I am getting you out of that nunnery! Mark, a friend of mine who has been living in New York, is moving to New Hampshire to live deliberately. This leaves his apartment vacant. I spoke to him about you and he said he'd tell his landlord that he should give the apartment to you. If all goes well you can have his room — it's in the West Village, there's a Murphy bed in the wall — as of November 15. Call the school at St. Frances Xavier on Sixteenth Street — or Fifteenth Street, I forget which — and ask for Mark Fitzgerald.

Love,
Bernard

PS. I got asked to leave the farm; I'll tell you about it later.
Write me in Boston when you write next.

October 30, 1958

Bernard —

Thank you. Thank you. I called Mark and went over and met with his landlord and I will be moving in with my books and percolator on November 15. This was the only time in my life that I was glad of being the weaker sex — I think my new Italian landlord is relieved to have what he imagines to be a proper lady occupying that room, and he gave me the place on the spot. A proper *Catholic* lady — I shamelessly asked Mr. Bellegia where I should go to Mass because I thought this might make him look favorably upon me. And I was right. It was just after this that he said the place was mine. I hope the Lord doesn't mind that I took his name in gain. I'd like to believe that the Lord thought I was being wise as serpents. Mmm. Probably not.

I like this neighborhood very much. I like the river, I like the gray and brick, I like the tumult of people on the crosshatching of narrow streets.

Your very grateful friend,
Frances Reardon

PS. What did you do?!

Frances —

Now you are a real New Yorker, cushioned no longer by mashed potatoes and the *muy* loco in loco parentis of the Barbizon. I salute you! Those winds off the Hudson are strong. Be warned. Will they blow you up my way? I wonder.

I am enclosing the proofs of your story. It should be in the spring issue. I am allowing you ten corrections in total. It's my policy: everyone gets up to ten corrections; more than that and the piece is pulled. I am imagining everyone as correction-mad as myself. This is why my book has taken this long to come out. I was on my fourth set of proofs when I saw you this summer. John Percy, my editor, has said that between the third and the fourth, the production department made a Wanted poster out of my author photo. I look forward to seeing this.

I have to come to New York in the next few weeks — am dropping off my pages. I can't wait for those winds to blow me your way — may I visit?

What happened at the farm is that they caught me and the novelist — the novelist was a girl — swimming without suits in the pond at night. The girl didn't mean anything to me, but they could not quite believe that. The girl was a little crazy; she had these huge eyes and was terribly thin, and whenever I looked at her I always felt she was trembling, but that was only an optical illusion brought on by the fact that she was talking incessantly, so much it made my teeth chatter, about being a vegetarian and Tolstoy and Gandhi and celibacy and a Russian professor of hers who was married and who kept writing her at the farm. "He is married," she kept saying while giving me a look that I was supposed to understand meant that he'd slept with her, or was trying to, and I could too, if I wanted to. I didn't do much to convince them I most certainly did not want to. The girl wanted to stay because she was broke and had nowhere else to go, and

I think they're going to keep her on, to take care of their daughter. Michael is probably a much better Christian than me — if I were as godly, I would not have decided to celebrate my last week of summer by swimming naked at night, but have you ever seen the moon waxing crescent, hanging low and white in the sky, and heard the breeze blow through the bushes and trees? You feel as ripening and shining as the night you are in, and it's excruciating to stand there enduring nature — God's instantiation, God's invitation — as a spectator when you can plunge yourself in the middle of it. That felt sinful, to not plunge myself in the middle of it. It made me think of Augustine:

> God, then, the most wise Creator and most just Ordainer
> of all natures, who placed the human race upon earth as
> its greatest ornament, imparted to men some good things
> adapted to this life, to wit, temporal peace, such as we
> can enjoy in this life from health and safety and human
> fellowship, and all things needful for the preservation
> and recovery of this peace, such as the objects which are
> accommodated to our outward senses, light, night, the air,
> and waters suitable for us, and everything the body requires
> to sustain, shelter, heal, or beautify it: and all under this most
> equitable condition, that every man who made a good use of
> these advantages suited to the peace of this mortal condition,
> should receive ampler and better blessings, namely, the
> peace of immortality, accompanied by glory and honor in
> an endless life made fit for the enjoyment of God and of one
> another in God —

Light, night, the air, and waters suitable for us. That was what was in front of me, and I felt that I should make good use of them.

I quoted this passage to Michael as explanation, but he said I was perverting the text. That I was out of my mind to think that the passage legitimized my pagan gesture. I quoted Paul to him — you know, if you want to eat meat, eat meat; if you don't, don't, etc. — and then he said that my concept of sin was too precious and he quoted Paul back to me by reminding me that I was living according to the flesh, that I was too alive to sin and too dead to Christ. (Yes, the girl added luster to the evening, and I'll confess to you that maybe I liked that there was something Edenic about the two of us in the water, and it occurred to me that I was indeed too alive to sin in that moment, but I was not interested in making anything more of our nakedness than a picture in my mind.) Michael and I went on for an hour, quoting scripture back and forth to each other, voices getting louder, which brought Eliza to the shed. She entered the room like Yul Brynner inspecting the slaves' quarters or some such in *The Ten Commandments* (now I'm infected with your disdain, goddamn you) and put her hand on my arm, and while her touch was just a touch, just four fingers on my forearm, it put silence into me, because she was also looking at me with cold iron-gray-blue eyes, and then she said: "I think you are too great a disturbance to this house," and asked me to leave. Ted thinks she got her moral authority purely from the fact that she'd thought I'd harassed a girl, not because I'd sinned. I laughed, but I think he's wrong. Mostly.

Do you know we have now been writing to each other for just over a year?

Love,
Bernard

November 17, 1958

Bernard —

Thanks for the proofs. I have availed myself of all ten permissible corrections. I hope that rewriting a paragraph counts as a correction. Because four out of the ten are that. The rest was correcting what your proofreaders should have corrected. But I know you're corralling glamour-seeking Harvard grads to do that stuff, so I can't expect them to actually give a rat's ass about doing their work. I think I smelled gin on these pages. Were these proofread at a cocktail party?

Bernard. You do realize that you have been kicked out of two Catholic communities for what looks like an inability to control yourself around women? I trust you left this out of your account because this goes without saying? I guess I should bring up Augustine again to scold you — you are still pre-conversion! — but this makes me laugh. Part of me thinks Ted just may be right. I like to think of your excesses as God visiting a judgment on these people's fervor. That you have come to show them that the Church is the only house that could gather us sinners together in peace.

Please do come to visit my Catholic community of one. There are no chores except for making coffee and washing five dishes. Is this labor purging enough for you? I now have a small wooden table that I picked up off the street, with two wooden chairs, and I have taught myself how to make crepes. I have made them for my office mates — there was a small fire at the end of the evening when one Peter from publicity tried to turn a few into a flambé with his bottle of whiskey, and some of my bangs got singed off. But I stand undaunted with my spatula and would love to make some for you.

Yours,
Frances

November 27, 1958

Frances —

Yes, I do realize why I have gotten, as you say, kicked out of those two Catholic communities. I pray every day to have a calmer heart. I have been praying to the Holy Spirit. I'm not ashamed, but I am confused as to why this keeps happening. Why I go blank to reason, to self-control, to the purity God asks of me. Why I think I am doing the thing God wants me to do. Why I would not feel ashamed for him to find me in the middle of what I am doing. I take comfort in Paul: I do the things I do not want to do, and never do things I know I should. I take comfort also in Augustine, it's true: the long, slow grudging, confused progress to God. The detour through the sin he thought was light.

I take comfort in the fact that you have borne with me.

I hear that the *Paris Review* wants to do an interview with me on the occasion of the publication of my book. It's supposed to be a conversation on how the classics have informed my work (their phrasing). I would rather they talk about how Catholicism has informed my work, because that is the real story, but the *Paris Review* doesn't know what to do about God taken up in earnest by someone who is not a demagogue or a rube. They are sending a young Barnard grad up to Boston to do it. They are doing a bright-young-things issue, and it appears that I am one of their favorites. I told them that you are one of my favorites. I sent them a copy of your story.

What are you doing for Thanksgiving? There is no avoiding going home for dinner. It will involve aunts and uncles and cousins, and soup tureens, and heirloom silver, and ivory linens scalloped at their edges with yellowing lace, and my mother will sit next to my father, who will be at the head of the table, and castrate him with a dozen nearly imperceptibly cutting remarks, some of which he will laugh at because, although he will sense that he is being demeaned, he will not have the strength of intelligence necessary to seize on the nature of the complaints. He needs my mother to anchor him and make him feel that he has done his duty as a man. Which is: to marry someone suitable and fill the house his forebears have had possession of since the eighteenth century with his own family. Having done this, he has felt free to float indefinitely in the uneventful heaven of middle mercantilism, falling further and further asleep into the past, where my mother was tempestuous but not yet sour. "Is it time for feeding?" he'll say, walking into the kitchen, where my mother and my aunts will be furiously battening down the hatches. Few will have read, and no one will have understood, my book. "Bernard," my mother will say, "these poems do give me a headache. But I trust that the people in New York know what they're doing." My father will not have read them at all. He will feel threatened by them, because even though he does not care for the life of the mind, he knows that somewhere in the life of the mind, his son is a success in a way he never was, and he paid for all the education, but he never meant for the education to mean anything; for him, Harvard was a convention to be observed the way church was a convention for my mother. But he enjoys feeling me out for poverty to see if he can't compromise me with an offer of his money. I've caught him inspecting the bottoms of my shoes for holes. Back to dinner. If my grandmother were still alive she would say that it's a good thing my mother didn't have a girl because any girl my mother had would have had to spend her whole life in exile from the dessert table. And then she'd cut me an extra-large slice of pie. My uncle George will ask me why I'm not wearing a collar if I'm a priest, and I will have to remind him again that I didn't end up going to seminary. And he will say, like he always says, that I'm much better off that way because I know the Catholic Church is filled with greasy, immigrant blood-drinking pagans, don't I, and it would be like serving a mission in Africa if I had to pastor that herd. This is my father's brother. His daughter, my cousin Caroline, however, will ask me about my teaching and tell me that she will try to read my book, and I will ask her about her teaching and then try to remember if I have met any young men who are tender enough for her. Caroline teaches kindergarten at a progressive school in Boston — she's an Alcott daughter brought up by bankers. She has Walden Pond in her eyes but some schoolmarm in her heart, so she won't stray too far from the Eliot ethos, which is mulish pursuit of respectability and material comfort. She and Ted once had an abortive, though charming, interlude that ended because Ted needs a little less Walden Pond and a little more Mediterranean tempest, and she needs a little less crank and a little more complacency.

Are you going home for Thanksgiving?

As you might say: Who is this Peter?!

Yours,
Bernard

December 5, 1958

Bernard —

Who is this Peter?! Bernard, I sigh. And then laugh at you and your persistence in imposing romance where there is none. Peter is a young man with whom I work. He likes whiskey and Edmund Burke. That is all I can tell you. When I find out that I really am in love with him, the bastard, in spite of myself, I will let you know. Dear God.

In return: How sharp and fetching was the Barnard grad?

Thanksgiving was pleasant. I went home on the train and helped my aunts make dinner, as I have always done. There are so many of us there need to be Sterno cans on the dining room table. This year I was in charge of the pies. All seven of them. I made a mincemeat pie for my father, which he ruined by eating a slice before it came out from behind the wings. Mincemeat is a pie for old people. My cousins and their children vastly preferred the whipped chocolate cream cheese pie, the recipe for which I got off the back of the Ann Page cream cheese package. This is slumming for me, the supermarket directive, but I do sometimes — sometimes — want to please a crowd. So as to better camouflage my dissent. My father raised a glass to my book being turned in, and everyone loudly cheered. I wanted to hide. There's an aunt and an uncle who show up in the book as a battle-ax and the stone that ax loves to grind itself on, but I doubt they'll read it. Or if they do, I bet they won't be able to recognize themselves as two old nuns. A cousin said she was glad to see that I hadn't gotten uppity since I moved to New York. I said I was glad I hadn't gotten sold into white slavery. But it was a fine time in general.

Thank you for sending my work on to those people. Never expect more than a handful of people to understand what you are about when you are writing about God. Or care.

Your immigrant blood-drinking pagan friend,
Frances

December 8, 1958

Bernard —

So I have had a talk with my agent about my editor. I can't take it anymore. This woman is dead set against mystery. She is asking me to articulate why things are happening when they are happening. She is asking me to explain what I want the reader to realize by accumulation. "Why is Sister John so mean?" she says. "I don't understand it. You need to tell us why." She won't bring herself to tell me to give the book a happy ending but she is talking around it. I think she thinks I can turn the book into *The Nun's Story*. She says that if I want to persist in my obscurity — she calls it obscurity — then I can go to one of those smaller houses that print difficult books.

She should not have put that thought into my head.

I do not like to ask favors of people, but threats to my work make me lose all scruples, and I have to protect my book. I humbly ask: Is there any way that you might speak to John on my behalf?

My gratitude to you.

Yours,
Frances

Dear John —

I got the copies of the book. It looks wonderful. I don't, however. In that author photo I look like someone told me to think of Aristotle's *Poetics* and then, on the count of three, snapped the picture. Why did I not see this before? Why did you not mention this to me? My mother might have told me as much but I still can't hear her when she tells me I'm being stubborn, selfish, or smug. Oh well. That's the least of my worries, this picture. All that matters is what's on the pages, and I can find no fault there.

Thank you for getting production to make those last changes. Book publishing is depressingly bureaucratic. And philistinic. I don't see how you can stand it. I can barely stay awake in faculty meetings. People have discussions about pedagogy. They delect in the hashing out of various ways to programmatically open the mind and consolidate insight. "Well," I said one day when one discussion had stopped at a crossroads that had been reached by a painfully democratic and glacially moving airing of multiple but finally identical methodologies, "the Greeks thought you could get pretty far with pederasty." The chair sighed deeply. I had forgotten where I was and said what occurred to me. Have you ever had the experience of being so bored that you feel only your eyes in your head? That you're only eyes, and the rest of you has diffused away into a roving gas? I don't imagine you have. That was the state I was in when I spoke. This is why you have the job you do, and I evaporate into a roving gas with eyes at whatever job I have. But I do love the students, and to get to the students I have to wade through a slough of middle-mindedness. It feels like wading through concrete fresh from the mixer. With the students, I experience one of the purest states of being I know. I can float into the classroom as that gas after some dreadful meeting, and then as we talk I solidify into wholeheartedness. Single-mindedness. As you know: Purity of heart is to will one thing. Everything — worry, anger, sloth, frustration — falls away in the talking. I feel God in the room in the pure exchange of ideas, and their awakening to ideas.

Speaking of middle-mindedness. Frances Reardon — the young woman I told you about from the colony — needs a new editor. I think her house is more grown over with bureaucracy and philistinism than yours, and her book needs you. Her editor, who took over the book after Frances's original editor left to marry a banker, sent the manuscript back to her with only ten marks on it, seven of them arbitrary deletions, and a letter in which this editor asked if Frances could lessen the religious themes, because they might be off-putting, and said that she didn't know whether she should like the protagonist or not, which was bothering her. I think her editor is a girl who has her job because she is tenacious and vapid — the tenacity masking the vapidity, and the vapidity fueling her ascendancy because vapidity frees the mind from bothersome, cumbersome self-examination. Let me know what we can do.

Yours,
Bernard

December 16, 1958

Frances —

I've written to John about you. He's going to get in touch with your agent.

I'm sending you a copy of my book. With all my love. I wonder what you will think of it. Whatever judgment you deliver will be God's grace.

Yours,
Bernard

December 20, 1958

Bernard —

I want to thank you for getting me out of the nunnery and possibly getting me out of this other house of horrors.

And: thank you for your book. It's handsome. But please do not mistake me for someone who has direct communication with God. Also, I'm a fiction writer. My judgments are the judgments of a mortal, and they are hobbled by my earthbound obstinate insistence on the concrete. You know what I've told you before. You and I are so very different: I am one word at a time, one foot in front of the other, slowly, always testing how sure my footing is before proceeding to the next sentence, with ruminative breaks for buttered toast and coffee. Your poems make the old feeling of cowdom come over me: stalled in a vast unconquerable field, alone, ruminating. While you're Christopher Wren. You've made me commit the grave sin of hyperbole in trying to convince you of my esteem — Christopher Wren! Dear God. So be flattered.

Yours,
Frances

January 15, 1959

Dearest Claire —

Happy new year!

Well, it seems that I will now be edited by John Percy at Harrow, through the intervention of Bernard. Bernard would want to say it was God who arranged it all, but I am content to leave it at his creatures' human kindness. That said, it does feel a certain blessing, to be rescued from the blind. John reminds me of Bill. Right down to the plaid work shirts. Only John does not safety-pin the cuffs back on when they wear themselves off the sleeves. I kept wanting to tell John about the time Bill pinned his wrist to the shirt accidentally, but John has a bit of primness about him, and I was trying to pretend that I was a Serious Artist.

This has made me indescribably relieved, but I am worried about something. I read Bernard's book of poems, and Claire, I am afraid that while Christ is all over these poems, hidden in historical figures, alluded to, quoted, and then expanded on as a way to reach Bernard's own impressive imagery, Christ is not really in these poems. He is too on the surface of them to be actually moving within them. I do not doubt that Christ is in Bernard — and very deeply. When Bernard speaks of the Church he speaks of it with humility and passion. But Christ is buried — in Bernard's poems and in his heart — under striving for world-historical Meaning and Complexity. I hear, in the poems, shields and lances clanking against the limitations of this imperfect world. Christ being the shield and lance — Bernard's weapon against nihilism. I fight that war myself. This is why Bernard is necessary to me. But I also think the symbolism is a cover for what Bernard might really want to talk about, which is his own history. He is encoding his own struggles with purity, desire, and despair in the symbols of religion, and then sometimes the Greeks, for good measure. (What do I know about the Greeks? I know what I know mainly from Aquinas. Bill could read these and tell us for sure.) I wonder if a better weapon against nihilism might be one man's life. One man in a struggle, and in that one particular struggle we more clearly apprehend the real. I suppose that is why I write fiction: character as argument. I suppose that is why I love Augustine. And Kierkegaard: one man in a war against despair directing us in our own hobbling away from it.

Also from Aquinas: the intellect is God present in his creation. The intellect should be a servant to revelation, but Bernard is thinking that the intellect itself, amassed on the page, is revelation.

I suppose I should write these things to Bernard. I don't know why on this occasion I find myself unable to say what I think. You and I could not be friends if you had not told me that I needed to stop being so silent in workshops, and I had not told you that if you did not marry Bill you would be a fool. I don't think what I am saying could possibly put a dent in him. Bernard's self-confidence is as impervious as a redwood. My words will be as the gnawing of a squirrel at its base. He can't hear things — in the way that he can't hear that it's his own confusion, not Christ's voice, speaking through the poems. I doubt he could hear what I am saying. But at least I will have said it. I feel obligated to do so.

Do I think, all this aside, that what he has done is beauty amassed on the page? I am not saying that he is a genius, but I do think that genius has something to do with mass and velocity, and the sheer torrent of words, the prolixity, the constant barrage of image and Shakespearean syntax, all coming so effortlessly — this feels to me something like genius. Without a doubt. There is so much intelligence and force that it razes my own will to create. In the way that talking with Bernard can raze my will to speak. I couldn't write for a week after reading the book. But I know Bernard wants beauty and truth, and the truth is getting a little mangled by the whirring blades of his mind.

And now — I think, after writing this to you, I can write these things to Bernard.

Love,
Frances

February 11, 1959

Frances —

Thank you for your letter.

How I wanted you to love what I had done. That was very childish of me, wasn't it? I think I knew what you would think of it. I think I wanted you to tell me what you told me, which is why I referred to your judgment as God's grace.

But you do think it's beautiful, even while in error, and that means a great deal to me. I'm not ashamed of what I've done. I'm still pleased with it. To turn on it would be to despair over it, which, as you know, is a sin. And I have you as a reader. So that's joy. And this is just my second book. So there's hope.

Thank you for not referring to me in your critique as the Sounding Brass.

Love,
Bernard

February 15, 1959

Dear Bernard —

Please always remember this: that whatever else I think about your poems, I will also be thinking that they are beautiful. If I didn't make it as clear as I should have that I was honored to read them: I was honored to read them. Very, very honored. I'm a little ashamed, because your letter reminded me of the flak I used to get in workshops for not being as complimentary as I could be. At the time I couldn't give a rat's ass because I didn't care about anyone in the workshop but Claire. Now things are very different. I should have perhaps been a little less forceful in pressing my point of view.

February in New York City is the very heart of darkness. Spring seems as far away as Fiji. I am wondering — would you come to visit in the next few weeks to liven it up around here? If you come, we can talk more about your poems. The offices are cold. People are wiping at their noses and look as if they haven't slept or washed their hair in days. On Friday, I snapped at Sullivan when he asked me for the third time where he was supposed to go to lunch. I've been reading too much because it's too cold to go out. I've gone through three Hardy novels in two weeks.

But I have some good news. There is a prospect of getting published in the *New Yorker*. They have one story and want another. Although: a pox on the *New Yorker*. John was told that they already have a Catholic woman writer — probably Elizabeth Pfeffer, because I think she's published with them two or three times — with a story slated to run this year, and they don't know if they can have two Catholic women in it within twelve months, so either my story will bump hers or hers will bump mine, and they'll hold on to what I've given them if I let them. But the two of us are so very different, as you know — she does the domestic ecstatic — so there's no chance that publishing us in what they consider to be rapid succession will make it look like the Vatican has annexed the *New Yorker*'s fiction department and is using it as a back office for nihil obstating. Perhaps you or John should write and tell the *New Yorker* editors that several prominent Catholics refuse to believe I'm Catholic! Thank goodness that working in publishing has made me privy, and therefore inured, to the unrelenting boneheaded arbitrariness that is supposed to pass for good taste. Thank goodness I at least have the stamina to write around a job. And, ahem, *at* the job. When Sullivan dies, I am in trouble. If they keep me, they might decide to give me to someone who actually needs my help.

Please do come and visit. I will bake you a cake that I have been itching to conquer.

Yours,
Frances

February 20, 1959

Frances, dear —

I would love to plunge with you into that heart of darkness. Alice and Tom will put me up. I'll be in on the Friday night train on March 6. Is that too soon? Or too far away? I'll call you when I get in.

Frances, my *dearest* dear, don't trouble yourself so much about the

New Yorker. There's room for everybody when the work is at your level. Actual talent keeps the doors opening. If they don't take your story, John or your agent will make sure some other periodical of repute does. And you have that job, which makes this even less of a problem, because you are not dependent on the *New Yorker* to increase either people's awareness of you or your bank account. (For now — like I said, you need to be looking for a husband with a steady income and a passing interest in books. Someone like Ted. If he hadn't squandered himself on Kay, I'd already have married you off to him.) You have me, you have John, and you have your agent, whose name I am always forgetting, and your work is a miracle. Don't be surprised if the *New Yorker* ends up publishing the housewife. Think about it: your sorority sisters from the Barbizon subscribe! But don't be troubled about it either. I have never published there, as you know. I doubt I will. Just write what you need to.

Your Bernard

February 27, 1959

Dear Bernard —

March 6 is too far away! But I can make it until your visit. I feel a little less trapped in my own garret now because the weather has warmed just a little, and I have awoken to the sound of birds. Actual birds! Where are they coming from? I dare not ask.

Well, I thank you for your words of encouragement re the *New Yorker.* That seems about right. (But: Oh, Bernard. A miracle? This is always the difference between you and me.) I do feel lucky having John now as my editor. I feel a certain amount of security and confidence about my (near) future because of it. But Bernard, I am compelled to remind you that you are successful enough to have a constant stream of teaching offers and so can turn down the money your parents are always offering you. This isn't envy talking, it's the desire to put your nose in the face of the facts, which you often push to the margins. Irish girls from North Philadelphia can't afford to think that they will be fine without the benevolence of the *New Yorker,* even as they give the *New Yorker* a Bronx cheer. And if I get wind of the fact that I am up against someone — oooh, I hate to lose. I really hate to lose. Especially when I know I'm the better bet.

I do have your friendship, though, and this Irish girl from North Philadelphia is quite grateful for your benevolence in extending it.

Yours,
Frances

Dear Frances —

I still don't know whether I should apologize to you or whether you should apologize to me.

I did not come to New York intending to kiss you. It happened because there was one moment in a boisterous, warm, convivial bar full of laughter, one moment containing one boisterous, almost wicked smile that I thought might have been because of me, or intended only for me, and I couldn't help myself.

I feel so very much for you and I wonder what it means. I have always felt this way — from the beginning — and now I wonder if I have been lying to myself about what it is that I feel.

I know this will make you even angrier than you were after I kissed you, but I often find myself wanting to call you my love. My love. Two words. Because you smile down the subway car at some waving child on a lap as we tunnel through thunder. You stand riveted in front of a Turner at the Met while tourists clog the room, and you mindlessly straighten your blue skirts as if they were hounds rustling at your feet waiting for the next command. You stare out the kitchen window while you do supper's dishes, making up comic-strip stories about the windows across the alley. I think this is partly why I want to call you my love: you are not turned inward.

Would it insult you or be a relief to you if I describe what I did as mere reflexive male jealousy? I could lie and say I did it because you had been talking too long to Peter. You have a great deal of pride, but it would not be insulted that way. You would probably be relieved if I said that, because it would mean I did it out of spite, out of sport, and not because I desired you. This makes me hate you a little. Because I have pride too, and I want to feel that you want me or need me. Because I need you. And I don't know who you would ever need. You wrote a letter asking me to come see you, making it clear that you wanted my company in particular, but I think deep down you don't really need anyone. If you did, you would have fallen in love with someone by now. That's not an insult. That is a thought that came to me as I wrote. I don't mean it as an insult. I haven't been in love with anyone, really, either. Everything's fallen apart. But I know I need people. You don't know how to need people.

If we say we love each other, what does it matter? It does not mean that we have to marry each other. It means only that we need each other, that we look out for each other. That our lives without each other would be less. And it's because I love you that I'm writing you this letter. I do think God sent you to me. I have plenty of people to talk to about poetry, but I don't want to talk to anyone, not even John, about God and art the way I want to talk to you about God and art. I need to know that you have the things in mind that I have in mind. I have been misunderstood but you don't misunderstand me — at least intellectually. I think God sent me to you because Claire can't break you. I think she's tried, from what you tell me, but you two are too much like an old married couple now for your barbs to really rend the flesh. She's married, and has her own life to build. She will find it less necessary to carve out of you what needs to be carved out because she has someone else now who needs her knife. In the same way Ted isn't around to carve out what needs to be carved out of me because he's about to be married and has his own life to build. So I think you and I found each other at precisely the right moment.

You will probably refuse to write me or see me after you read this letter. But I believe in absolute honesty. I believe also that our friendship will withstand my confusion and your horror.

Bernard

March 15, 1959

Bernard, you have knocked some wind out of me, and I need to make sense of it.

Please don't write back to this letter. I'll write you a longer one when I'm ready. Anything I say now is going to sound like a gavel coming down on your head, and I have fondness for you, a great deal of it, so I have to go away to be as kind as I believe the Lord wants me to be here. That's something I've never felt, and perhaps my fondness for you has made me feel it: the conscious impulse to shut my mouth for Jesus's and/or another person's sake.

My life without you would certainly be less. That is one thing I know.

Yours,
Frances

March 31, 1959

Claire —

I hope you're well.

I'm writing to tell you something I still can't quite believe.

The Sunday before last, Bernard showed up in the city, unannounced. I was sitting in church before five o'clock Mass started — there were only about ten of us — and while sitting there, I felt a hand clap on my shoulder. It was Bernard. It was barely fifty degrees that day but he was not wearing a coat. He was wearing a blue seersucker jacket and a button-down shirt, with his tan corduroys held up by his braided leather belt. He was clearly enduring something beyond his usual dishevelment. There was a hole the size of a quarter in the knee of his right pant leg. His hair was standing up a half inch higher than usual, and his eyes were looking at me as if I were one tree of many in a forest. Scratches on his bare ankles — he had not put on socks with his oxfords. His fingernails were laced with grime.

He pushed himself into the pew, shoving me to the right with his hip. "Frances," he said. "Your landlord said you would be here."

I couldn't speak. I just stared at him. I knew something awful was going to happen but I didn't know what. I could not push my mind past a repetition of the phrase *Lord, have mercy. Lord, have mercy, Lord, have mercy, Lord, have mercy.* My mind resting in that one thought like a bike chain gone slack. He put his hand on my knee. I didn't know what to say, so I put my hand over his. "It's your birthday," he said, and he held my hand tighter.

Somehow I got some presence of mind. "Why don't we go outside and walk around for a bit?" I said. Then he said a very strange thing: "It's your birthday, your feast day, and this is why I have come. Today is the day of Frances Reardon, orphaned child of Brigid's isle, patron saint of frigid knees. Of unmet wishes, of idées fixes, of withering eyes, of docile guise." He had continued staring at me as if I were one tree in a forest of many, but after he delivered this speech his look sharpened into something cruel. I'd felt what he was saying to me was cruel, and the look confirmed it.

Then he stood and started walking up the outer aisle. He began to shout, and said even stranger things. He said that this place — meaning the church — was no better than a bar room. "This place is a place where the people come to drink," he shouted. "They drink to forget, to die to what is real, they slump over in prayer, drinking and drinking in remembrance of me." I sorely wished for the gift of fainting from shock. He went down the center aisle. "I am turning you out!" he said. Two women got up and hurried out of the church, and at this point I found the courage to get up and walk as fast as I could to find the priest. I walked back to the door that leads from the sanctuary to the church office, and there stood the priest, white head bowed, shrugging on his robe. It's always like seeing them in their underwear when you see them in their belted slacks and dress shoes. He looked up. I saw eyes that were younger than his hair, and I felt relief. I told him what was happening and he went out with me, and this small white-haired Irish man managed to wrestle Bernard to the ground. The organist, who is a statuesque, almost stout, redhead, helped the priest keep Bernard there. At least they did for as long as it took for me to run out and find a cop, who then called an ambulance. When I came back in, Bernard had of course escaped the bonds of the priest and the organist and was throwing missals everywhere. It took four ambulance attendants to get him on a stretcher. He bit one of them. And now Bernard is in a hospital outside of Boston. He has been there for nine days.

John Percy, who has been to see him, tells me the doctors say he suffered a manic episode. When I think about all I have known of Bernard, and what I have now read of his disease, I see how his illness has been lying in wait for him. It will come for him again, and again.

As far as John can tell, Bernard came down on the train that afternoon. He told me that Bernard rang him up shortly before he came to see me and told him some addled things. John said he called me to tell me this and was going to offer to come over because he had a bad feeling about Bernard but I had already left for Mass. Apparently Bernard told John that he had received a revelation in a church in Boston that I was a saint, that I was the only pure thing in New York City, couldn't John tell, couldn't John tell that there was light around me because I had not sinned, I had not been touched, that I knew the true purpose of the Church, I was its defender, I was not drinking the blood like milk, the host was solid food for me, that I was a saint and when my book was published everyone would know that. John has been to see Bernard and tells me that Bernard does not remember saying any of this. When John told Bernard what he'd said, Bernard groaned and put his face in his hands and did not speak for a long while. John asked me to go see him because he thinks if Bernard does not hear from me he will not do as well as he might. John Percy does not say much, so if he tells me this, I can be reasonably assured that it is a real possibility.

I have prayed for Bernard every minute of every day. I am going to see him this week. I am staying with his friend Ted and Ted's wife.

Still, I am very angry with him. Please pray for me that this anger dissipates, because I know it is not right to be angry when my friend is suffering. I am very angry with him because in his mania he has confused me with a saint. I itch writing that sentence. I am angry with him because he did something to me in his mind, something that now makes me wonder what else had been in his mind before he said what he did. It's making it very hard to write — to the point where I don't know what's weighing heavier on my conscience, the blank page that's resulting from my anger or the anger itself. I sit in front of the typewriter and type and then start looking out the window, worrying about Bernard and then fuming at Bernard. And so he's turned me into a crazy person too — he's led me into the realm of *what if* and *who's there*?

Love,
Frances

April 15, 1959

Dear John —

Your office called and told me you are in England for a few weeks on business. I hope all is going well with you, and you are enjoying your time there.

You asked me to tell you what happened when I saw Bernard.

Hospitals are horrible places, and this sort of hospital in particular — it's supposed to be expensive, but it feels like a dump.

I walked into the common room and there was a baseball game on — the sound of it like flies buzzing over the heads of the bodies slumped in vinyl padded chairs. Gray linoleum, navy blue vinyl. I had baked Bernard some chocolate chip cookies at Ted's apartment — Ted said that Bernard was starving and had been making the staff miserable in his loud complaining about the food. So I walked into this awful, cloudy, bruise-colored room and saw Bernard's big curly head over the collar of a cheap red velour bathrobe the color of port. "Bernard," I said to the back of his head, and he got up and came to me. He looked exhausted. The bathrobe hung on him like something shaggy and ancient, but he still looked regal, like a chieftain robbed of his scabbard. "Bernard," I said, and took his hand. "No, no, that's not enough," he said. He took the package out of my other hand, put it down on a chair, and then pulled me to him. He was right. That wasn't enough.

That over, we took our seats. We didn't say anything for a while. I smelled the smell of that place — stale, a film of body odor, dust. Ammonia at base. The baseball game droned. I didn't know what to say that wouldn't sound inappropriate in its smallness or patronizing in its sincerity. "I made you some cookies," I said, "because Ted said you had been inciting riots at dinner." Bernard smiled. But his smile came slower than it usually does, and I realized that he must be swimming through the Thorazine. I started to cry and he saw this. "Now I know you love me," he said.

I brought *The Tempest* and I thought I could read him some of it. I should have realized that perhaps this was not the best choice. After a while he asked me to stop. "Are you afraid of me, Frances?" he said. "No," I said. "I'm not afraid of you. I want you to get well."

"You waited too long to come," he said.

I said nothing. That seemed the gracious thing to do.

"Please pray for me," he said. I told him I had been praying for him all this time.

I saw his parents on my way out — I heard his mother arguing with the nurses. I think they had gotten confused about his schedule and she wanted to be allowed to see him even though visiting hours were over. I see where Bernard gets the fire in the gut to demand better institutional dining. He has her face too. "Watch my purse," she said in ill temper to a nurse bustling by. She's the pier and Mr. Eliot is the dinghy tied to it, bobbing away in oblivion. I suppose I should have introduced myself but I didn't think it would go well.

I'm going next weekend. I'll give you another report then.

Yours,
Frances

April 15, 1959

Dear Claire —

How are you?

I just wrote a letter to John Percy about my visit to Bernard in which I seem to have left out some of my more cowardly feelings. I know that many people think that their editors exist solely to absorb those kinds of feelings, but I would be ashamed if John thought that I was less than stoic, as he seems so stoic himself.

It was very difficult to see Bernard. He is being given a drug called Thorazine, which is an extremely powerful sedative that is supposed to prevent psychosis. This means that when you talk to him, there is often a pause of several seconds before he answers — it is as if you are a customer in a dusty old general store, and he's the mummified cashier who has to remember where he's put whatever it is you're looking for or whether he even has it. This drug also makes his hands tremble. This started at the end of the visit, when I was reading to him, and when it did, he looked at me helplessly, panicked, as if to say *I don't know what's happening but I know I don't want you to watch it happen.* He finally sat on them. I didn't know what else to do but kiss his head. "Perhaps I should be institutionalized more often," he said.

I have never, in my twenty-six years, seen anyone laid out in a casket — I was kept away from my mother's funeral — but looking upon Bernard in the hospital, I imagined it was not dissimilar. I have never seen anyone I was fond of that altered physically. He is gray and crumpled. His eyes are dull. It took all that I had to keep looking at him straight on. I was determined not to be a child in front of him.

On the way out I asked a nurse how often he was given the drug, and how. She looked at me warily, and then explained: He is stripped down, strapped to a table, and then injected four times, in four different places. I nodded, thanked her, and then ran into a ladies' room stall to hide until I regained my composure. What humiliation. I'd have killed myself by now, if this were me. Do I mean that? Let's hope we never find out. I can't believe I'm writing this, but this has made me somewhat glad my mother passed away when she did, because if she'd lived any longer she might have ended up in a place like that.

When Ted picked me up, I asked him to pull over at the first church we saw. He said of course. I went in and asked that my fear not render me helpless. I asked forgiveness for the anger I had toward Bernard. Then Ted drove us home and poured us each a martini. I said I wasn't sure I wanted one — it was three in the afternoon, and I thought I might try to get some revisions done — but he kept right on shaking and stirring. "You'll be no good to anyone if you don't," he said, and handed me a drink. "It doesn't make all that wine any less transubstantiated, if that's what you're worried about." I do feel grateful for Ted.

I'll end this letter here.

Love,
Frances

85

Dear Frances —

Will you smuggle me in more books next weekend? My mother did not bring me the Shakespeare I asked for — she brought some Agatha Christie and John Dickson Carr instead. "Your mind must be tired," she said, "and I don't think it'll do to be revving it up with Shakespeare. I know you won't watch television but I thought some whodunits might be entertaining."

I can't stand mysteries. In the same way I can't stand science fiction. Why pretend we're somewhere else? Forensics is a feint. Why distract ourselves from the eternal questions with set dressing? Salad dressing.

Would you mind bringing me copies of *Cymbeline* and *The Winter's Tale*? My mother offers one pudding and Ted another: Ted says there's no better time than losing your mind to cleave to the decencies and unremarkable sentences of the Victorian novel, sentences bearing plot to the reader like freight car after freight car carrying cargo to its destination in Leeds. The way he has described the work of Trollope and Gissing and Thackeray, I now want the oasis of decency and plain English the way I want a roast chicken: there is secret opulence in both. Ted says not to worry; if I like these books it doesn't mean I'll end up married like him. That broke my heart, to hear Ted already joking but not joking about the death that is marriage. Do you know I have never read *Vanity Fair*? In my mind I had confused it with your *Little Women,* but Ted assures me that it's only a girls' book if you think Becky Sharp is a role model. It's really a pirate novel, he says.

The people here are all crushed cigarette stubs of people. Bent, white, ashen, diminished. Myself included.

I sleep the way some people commit suicide.

The priest here is, as you might say, a perfect ninny. He gave me a book by Bishop Sheen. That made me go black for a day or two.

I started to think that maybe God is as small as the minds who love him blindly.

All there is to do here is sleep, read, eat, stare out the window, or write Frances a long letter.

I wonder if God is playing a joke on me — the girls here are caricatures of all the women I've been with, or wanted to be with. There's a girl with yellow braids and a severe brow who's always carrying a copy of *Imitation of Christ*; a dark-haired girl who touches my feet under the table at meals but ignores me in the hall; a girl with auburn hair who speaks to me only in puns. Now I think I know what the nunnery must have been like for you. The psychiatrist who's analyzing me will tell you that these girls are all variations on my mother. I don't want to believe him, because how could I have been so obviously Oedipal? Aren't we much more than a collective impulse to frustrate and be frustrated? But I wonder now if it's not free will but the unconscious that we have been given. I wonder what of your mother was encoded in you without your knowing; what of your life is a letter she wrote you that you have just opened and will take your whole life to read.

Love,
Bernard

May 15, 1959

Dear Frances —

Thank you for bringing me those books. How beautiful the sight of you in your green and white striped dress. I suppose you'd say I'm only saying that because I'm in a nut house, and you were the only person who had washed in a week and was not catatonic. But I am going to say it again: how beautiful. Like cream, like clover blossoms. Your face says so much in so little time, you let everything you're thinking bloom upon your face, and I can't think of anything else I'd rather watch than you pass through five moods in five minutes. What glorious weather.

I think you have forgiven me. Have you forgiven me?

It's three in the afternoon, between herdings to and from meals, and I'm finding myself in a moment where I needed to talk to someone I love. I don't talk much to the other patients here. I don't really want to talk to anyone here, for fear it is revealed just how deep the similarities are between me and the old woman who pops out of her window every day at noon crying *cuckoo* across the quad. The narcissism of small differences, I suppose. I am forcing myself to read, even though I have to fight to stay interested past the first few pages. I keep it up, even if an hour goes by between pages, because I don't want this drug to have the last word on the strength of my spirit. I need to prove to myself that I can willingly inhabit worlds other than my own.

I don't like to look at myself in the mirror either. I have aged overnight. Some days I look gaunt as El Greco's Saint James, others I look as bejowled as my grandmother. In general I appear as cratered and evacuated of sense as the moon. My hair annoys me. Full, unruly, standing at attention, suggestive of robust and hardy vegetation, it seems to me an accessory left behind from a costume I'd been renting out. I leave it uncombed as punishment for its mockery of my otherwise gelatinous state. The nurses are always trying to get at it.

But I am very glad to hear that John is delighted by the novel. This is a thought I have been returning to, because it brings me what feels like happiness.

I'll take my leave now. I only want to keep writing about how beautiful you are, and I do not want to risk your censure. How beautiful, and yet you suffer this Polyphemus groping for you from his dark cave.

Love,
Bernard

May 21, 1959

Dear Bernard —

I will see you in a few days, but I wanted you to have something to read in the meantime that wasn't a mimeographed sheet telling you what not to take with your orange juice. I want to get this in the last mail, so it will be short.

Please keep reading. I think that is a good idea. I wanted to tell you that I have been reading *Cymbeline* too — I've never read it, which I'm sure you can believe — and in fact I just finished it, so when I see you we will talk about it some. They say it's a clunker, but I do like this line, from the end: "Pardon's the word to all."

I think you look as kind as you have always looked.

Yours,
Frances

PS. Although I think you should let the nurses at your sagebrush. If only for your mother's sake. And maybe mine?

June 1, 1959

Dear John —

I hope this letter finds you still enjoying England. If you have found any books over there that merit looking into, would you let me know?

I told you I would write you again about visiting Bernard, so here I am. They're letting him out on the fifteenth, and it seems like he's going to stay with his parents for the rest of the summer before moving to New York to take a teaching job at Hunter College. I think this may be one of those times where even ineffectual parents are better than no parents at all. Bernard is just humbled enough now to accept their care, and they seem humbled enough to swallow their objection to his being Bernard instead of an obedient son.

He seems better. Although I have no idea what *better* means, in this context. I think what I mean is that he seems eager to leave the hospital and resume his life, and that the people who run the hospital are going to let him. I worry about him a little because I sense that he is afraid of himself — that he thinks of himself now as a loaded gun likely to go off at anytime without warning. All I can do is pray for him and try to make him laugh when I see him — and not mind how feeble those two gestures are.

I know Bernard would love to see you when you get back. Your letters have been cheering. If you want to make plans to visit him, let me know and Ted McCoy will drive us out.

Yours,
Frances

July 12, 1959

Dear Claire —

Do you know what heaven must be like? I mean, a child's conception of heaven — a place you dread being caught dead in because it must be everlastingly quiet and mirthless? It must be like Proper Boston. Which is where Bernard's parents reside. Every time I took a step in their house I swear I heard the china and silverware rattle — no doubt an alarm to let the ancient Proper Bostonians know that some Irish servant girl's descendant was trespassing on their grounds, possibly with the intent to burgle — and in the deep silence a grandfather clock ticked off every eternal second. The house looked like the Colonial-era period rooms I remember staring into at the art museum: mahogany chests sitting like thrones in every room, discreet whispers of pewter and white lace. Bernard's parents were perfectly civil, but they seemed to have no actual life in them. His mother asked questions but didn't seem to care how you answered, and his father fell asleep at the table just before coffee was brought out. Bernard then woke his father up by whistling through his fingers, which is how he said his father used to wake him up when he was a teenager. "Do you want to give your father a heart attack right now, Bernard?" his mother said, floating toward the table with the coffee tray in a haze of matriarchal serenity. I just let Ted and John make the small talk.

We spent much of the visit in their small backyard, which featured many handsome rosebushes. (I couldn't help but notice they did not look as bug-eaten as the ones my father always tries to get going in milk cans outside our front door.) I could not say for sure but I thought Bernard seemed rested and close to something like well. He said he was writing, and had written seventy pages of something that didn't seem a failure. He joked, he listened attentively, he pried some gossip out of John (no man hath greater love than this, that he lay down his scruples for his friend Lazarus). After half an hour or so he sent Ted and John away — "Go talk to my father about the war," he told them, and they obliged — and then I panicked, wondering if he was going to become romantic. He took my hand, brought it to his mouth, and kissed it with no small amount of grief. I stopped panicking and felt grief too. He kissed my hand even harder, and then eventually set it down on my knee without letting it go. "It's terrible," he said. "You answered a letter and befriended a monster." At this his mother arrived in the yard. She clucked her tongue and both of us looked up, startled. (I have never seen Bernard startled. He's usually the thing doing the startling.) "Stop that this instant," she said to him, and I noticed her chin trembling. "You are no such thing." Neither of us said a word. "Now, would you two like something to drink?" she said. By this time he had composed himself. I didn't think people's chins actually trembled, but hers did. "No, thank you, Mother," he said. And I could tell that he was pleased that she had intervened in some way on his behalf because of the note of gratified surprise in his voice. From what he's told me, that kind of protective, affectionate rap on the knuckles was rare. We were silent for a few moments, and then he began to stroke my hair, and I let him, even though I thought he might have been trying to push his luck. I didn't have the heart to crab about it. After a while Ted came into the yard and gave me a look that told me I was doing the right thing. "Time's up, Dante," he said. "I came back here because John was too nice to. Come on, reward us by rejoining the household."

Later there were another few minutes of panic. After lunch, when the men had gone out back to smoke their various tobacco items, I was left alone at the table with Mother Eliot. Who said, as if two hours hadn't gone by between the yard and lunch: "He's grown self-pitying. I'll have none of it." It's true that Bernard's penchant for exaggeration is trying, and it's true that I was glad she rapped his knuckles so I didn't have to, but her lack of compassion gave me the crazy thought that I needed to get him home so my aunts could swaddle his convalescence in good cheer. Before I knew what I was doing I heard myself replying: "If there was ever anything to be self-pitying about, losing your mind might be it." She gave me a look that chilled my blood. At the time I thought it chilled my blood because it did not differ much from the looks Bernard gave me that day in March. There was a kind of glazed fire behind her eyes, and it wiped out any sense that she was speaking to another human being, let alone a human being who had a point worth considering. But now I'm not sure I saw what I thought I did.

I was glad to be in a car with Ted and John shortly after that. Although Bernard did seem very happy to see us. And I was happy to see him that way.

So that is the news. That and the tops of my feet are peeling something fierce because I went out to Rockaway Beach for the day with a girl from work and I forgot to put Coppertone on them. Send me some of your news, and soon.

Love,
Frances

July 12, 1959

Dear Frances —

So now you have seen the Eliot manse. What did it look like through your eyes?

I felt so lucky to have the three of you here. Did you notice the way John gave up the gossip on Carl and Nancy? I actually think John rather enjoyed setting that story out — the way his smile grew deeper and ever more sly at each piece of information he divulged it was as if he were proudly spreading caviar over a very long loaf of pumpernickel for us all.

I think I need to apologize for petting your hair as I did. I do, don't I?

What is there to say? I miss you already. Now what. My mother is trying to get me to quit smoking by throwing out the packs of cigarettes she finds lying around the house. There are many, because I lose them moving from bedroom to kitchen to yard and I have to buy more to replace them, and so on and so forth. She didn't like you, I have to say. I find this amusing. "Where did you meet that girl again?" she said yesterday, and I could hear the rest of that thought hanging in the air: *It surely wasn't Smith College.* I think she can tell that you take pains not to know your place, and she wants to know who or what encouraged this wildness. I think she can also tell that I love you for it.

I'm glad to be recovering in the summer. Isn't that silly? I've lived most of my life on an academic schedule, so I am used to being set loose to loaf during these months. I can pretend that being set loose to recuperate is not that different. And there are many other people on furlough from their lives now — I can tell myself that I have not fallen too far out of step with the rhythms of reality.

Now that I am off the drug, I can sit in the sun. I come out in the garden every day to celebrate this fact. My mother has just opened a window to tell me to put some zinc on my nose. It is noon now, and

I think I may be out here until the sky ripens into a peach-bottomed plum, just because I can.

I would have prayed to be delivered from that drug if I'd had the ability to conceive of words that expressed preference, or hope. I didn't care that I wasn't writing because I didn't care about anything. That was similar to what I'd felt during various depressions — words always out of reach. Words on a shelf too high for my lazy, faithless arms; words blurred and smeared around the sides of the errant crucible that was my mind; words a thing I had been smitten with now betraying me with their dullness. But this was worse. My mind was a ball of steel wool and lard.

When they took me off the drug, I had a few panic attacks, it appears, waiting for my will to return. I did not think it would. But here I am, at my parents' house, sitting in the sun, in their yard, writing you. I don't feel cured, but I do feel glad to go to bed without wishing for sleep to extinguish me. I did not think that was possible. I see that I may have my family in me after all — the other day my father said that everyone's been concerned for my health, but "no one likes a layabout." I would never have said a thing like that, but I am interested in, I am committed to, as he might say, moving along. It's not unlike the difference between nausea and health: when you're well you can't imagine what it's like to be ill, you've forgotten the exact dimensions of the squirming lassitude, and when you're ill, you pant for wellness, whose sturdy contours now seem the unimaginable thing. The sane you, the real you — it must have been real, why else the innumerable vivid scenes of leaving your house and ending up exactly where you intended, of speaking swiftly and unselfconsciously and being understood, of being enchanted by small joys, your own and others'? You know it must have been real, but now you are not so sure — that dependable, uninterrupted flow of thought and action now seems a fiction, not your broken mind. But here I am in the yard. Here are birds. I'm writing, and I've written more than I thought I would. The neighbors' sweetly rotund daughter is making a halting mess of Schumann on the piano. And now a church bell comes in, tolling "This Is My Father's World," and she gives up the Schumann to play along with hygienic Sunday school zeal. I want to tell her that may be a wise choice, to take refuge from one of the most Romantic of the Romantics in the orderly march of hymns. I close my eyes, then open them, and the scene is fixed; it does not spin or buckle. I close my eyes, then open them, and: the same. So I keep on writing.

Frances, you too are fixed for me, you do not spin. You won't again, if I can help it.

Neither one of us really wants to speak of what happened now that we are in the light, I can tell, and I think that's best. Here is one case, Frances dear, in which I am glad of your reticence. I've spent enough time lately trying to figure out how my parents, and their parents, and their parents, etc., created the conditions that led me to the hospital. In the beginning I was glad of the chance to blame. When it comes to blaming one's parents, everyone loves the feel of a lighted torch in the hand, especially when it appears that torch is being handed to you by a Harvard-laureled practitioner of one of the West's great interpretive frameworks. But that flame died quickly and I felt crushed by the weight of my parents' blindness. I now feel sorry, somewhat, for my mother and father. I'm trying to feel sorry for them so that I don't feel sorry for myself.

Don't feel sorry for me, or afraid of me. Please remain my friend.

Love,
Bernard

July 20, 1959

Dear Bernard —

I was very much moved by your letter.

I will of course remain your friend.

What did I think of the Eliot manse? Well, it was impressive in the way it came off as both austere and lavish. Should there ever be a Marxist revolution on American soil, your parents will be safe, as their people taught them how to hide in plain sight. But really and truly, I was most jealous of your mother's splendiferous roses. If I one day happen to have a yard all my own, splendiferous rosebushes will be the first order of business. The yellow ones were my favorites — pale and frothy, as if they would smell of eggnog and not roses.

Let's just say that your mother and I seem to have decided that we will not have a mutual admiration society.

You're right — I do feel hesitant to talk about what happened. My people, for better and for worse, taught me how to hide what was too difficult to bear. I feel shy as I write to you. I don't want to say anything that's beside the point. One of the things I want to say I know is childish, but I mean it with my whole heart: I hope you never have to take Thorazine again.

I want you to feel hope more than you feel despair. That is what I have been praying for.

Yours,
Frances

July 30, 1959

Frances, my dearest dear. My mind might be a little potholed right now, but I think my heart is as sturdy as ever. Don't handle me lightly. Tell me what you're thinking.

I have a feeling that after you read this you're going to take me at my word, and with a vengeance.

When I read your letter and thought about you praying for me, I felt that I needed to confess some thoughts to you. I have been thinking — it is all I can do here — and you are the only person to whom I can write these thoughts. You won't like them, but I have to confess them to you.

Do you remember what you wrote about Simone Weil? How she wrote that it's sort of humorous, the line "Our father, who art in heaven"? I am beginning to see that it is indeed humorous. That it is ludicrous. That I was deluded in my imagining that I could communicate with him. I think you, rightly, keep this in mind as a way of remaining humble, of purging your faith of craven obedience — if he can't answer you, he can't hold anything over you. I wanted to have this sort of humility and patience myself. Now I think I never did, and so perhaps I really never did receive him.

I have been thinking about the letter you wrote to me after the book came out. You did not say that I was poetizing my love for God, but I see now that's what I was doing. I wonder how deeply his word had a place in my life. I wonder how deeply he had worked his way in. I wonder what I was doing when I was praying. When the abbot saw me — now I see what he saw.

Who was I praying to? Was I straining, and did the straining lead to silence? Did my straining serve only myself? I wanted to feel something. So I trumpeted loudly, waiting for the selfishness in me to fall. Another Old Testament metaphor: I built myself a god who was not God, who was only myself made boundless. When I review all the things I did while I thought I was in the throes of what I might have called the Holy Spirit, I see everything I did as one more gold earring tossed into the fire. My fervor was self-adornment.

When I think about all my fervor, and realize that God is an image thrown up by my illness, it's very hard for me to understand my faith as anything other than a fever dream. Especially when I am said to have said what I did during my episode. Faith is now inextricably linked to madness for me. This is a great sorrow. I wish very much for you to believe that it is a great sorrow.

I will never be the sort of person who despises religion.

And my faith also might have been fueled by a great fear — I wanted an ancestry that would not be the meaningless ancestry of my family: blood, land, money. I wanted a lineage, and what better church in which to seek a lineage?

So all of this is seeming very much like fear, obstinacy, vanity, and illness.

To go on in it would be like going on in a marriage after one discovers unfaithfulness. I know some people would dig in to the marriage, would fight for what they believed to be the truth about the marriage, which was that it was a good thing that has been wounded, and they would use their love to stanch the flow. But I see the uselessness of that kind of love now — that love may not be love, but fear. I could not stand under God now with a pure, expectant heart. After all that's happened, I think my heart still has something pure and hopeful in it — if it didn't I wouldn't be writing you. But I don't want to think that there's a supernatural tone whose object is to extract purity from me. I went back and read Augustine last week and his own need for God is his own need for God — I am not moved. I am moved by the tenderness with which he comes to philosophic problems of memory, of time, and metaphors of creation, but I do not feel moved to capitulate as he capitulated. I once met a former priest — turned atheist by the war — who told me that every time he read the *Confessions* he found himself lured back to a desire for belief because of Augustine's description of a God who would not give up on us. But I am utterly immune to the chords he's playing.

I am sorry.

Love,
Bernard

Dear Bernard —

I wrote two other versions of this letter but then I decided to proceed as if your heart is indeed as sturdy as you say it is.

If you're so focused on your own selfishness — your own sin — you will of course lose your faith. If you concentrate on your need for faith as display, you will never find him.

This is more attention paid to self, the notion that because you were selfish, your love was never really love. I have heard you speak, Bernard. And even though I will agree with you and say that yes, occasionally I thought exactly what you have said — that God was sometimes merely a conduit for feelings and thoughts that were too large even for your poems — I never, ever thought that you were deluding yourself in a love of him. Or that you were acting. I saw you as someone who was truly trying to love God.

A word on parishioners: Parishioners are not Christians. They are parishioners. Their allegiance is not to God but to their priest, whom they think is God. It's like *Heart of Darkness* with Kurtz. And often priests are not Christians either, because they have too much of Kurtz in them. When a friend of mine was about fourteen, she found herself followed around the neighborhood by a young man who'd recently been discharged from the army after he'd had a nervous breakdown. He was the son of a man who owned a large grocery store and who gave a lot of money to the church school. The young man's attentions were troubling my friend, and when it got to the point where he parked his car outside her house one night with the lights off, her father went to the priest and asked him to talk to the family about it. The priest said that it would be impossible to bring this up because it might offend the man whose generosity kept the church's mission going. This man's generosity was necessary, but the safety of my friend was not. My friend's father eventually moved them a few towns over to get away from this boy. I am enraged by stories like this, and I've heard many of them. But if I decided to let this be the last word on God's nature I would be no better than this priest who decided to let the supermarket king define what charity was. There is the church and there is the Church.

As far as loving your neighbor, you have always done a better job of that than I have, or ever will. Please do not berate yourself for not inventing the Catholic Worker.

I wonder if you should meditate some on the idea that God is eternal and bides his time. You once wrote to me of taking Augustine's slow, blind journey to belief as an example. I am praying for you to see once again that we will never be made perfect in this lifetime, and that's how God wants it. Perfection is what comes after this lifetime. You know your Paul. So you should know this.

If God is eternal he stands outside your illness. He cannot be corrupted by it.

Also, I think that psychoanalysis is reinforcing whatever selfishness you think you are crippled by. If you say you are suffering from a wish to be a hero, and that this wish has corrupted your faith, I don't see how this system will disabuse you of that wish. It seems to me that it will keep putting you front and center of your own myth. Why is the unconscious any better than free will? What does it serve us to imagine ourselves enslaved to impulses? If you never imagined that we were enslaved to sin, why imagine that we are enslaved to drives and paralyzed by frustrations that we had no hand in making? This seems like nihilism.

I'm sending you this prayer to Saint Anthony that I hope might prick your conscience. I realize how much that makes me sound like my aunts and the nuts who buy Bishop Sheen's books. But I am willing to take up the weapons of spiritual warfare used by the Irish banshees of Kensington if it means you might come back to the fold.

Love,
Frances

Dear Frances —

The card with Saint Anthony on it is now in my wallet. I intend it to stay there for all time.

Nevertheless, I can't help what I am thinking and feeling now. These thoughts and feelings are truths piling up like rocks against the deluge of my previous whims; they feel like something to build from. Whatever I thought I knew scatters and drifts when I ask myself: Who and what did all this performance serve? I think this is perhaps the first time in my life that I can be said to know my own mind. I wish this acquaintance could have been made in a less disastrous way, but I am glad of it nevertheless. And there is still something in me that wants to say God has orchestrated this revelation. See, Frances, I am no complacent, smugly Buddha-minded, excessively rational indifferent atheist. Don't worry, I won't say Freud's the orchestrator here.

I don't want this parting of practice to sever our friendship. Am I naive to think it won't? I still want you to make me laugh, and I want to make you laugh, and I want to read your work and see how it is coming into being, and help you strengthen it if you want me to, and I want you to take your pen to my work and see on what points I might be silent. I want the ruthlessness of your last letter riding my work to bits. When I look at you without my faith, I still see you, Frances, shining-eyed, penetrating, sound-hearted. I know that what you love me for is not God within me but me — or am I also naive in thinking that you did love me for me? It would fill me with sorrow to think that you and I could not ever again walk by the Hudson together and talk until the sun went down. We may not ever take communion together like we did that August, or that March, but could we not make New York City our sanctuary?

Write when you feel you can.

Love,
Bernard

Dear Bernard —

I have been thinking about faith, and your faith, and what might be helpful for you to hear at this moment. You might not want to hear about what I've been thinking, and it might sound hollow to you, but just write me and tell me if so. I've told you when I haven't wanted to hear from you, so maybe it's time I have a dose of my own medicine.

I think often of this sentence from Kierkegaard: "It is beautiful that a person prays, and many a promise is given to the one who prays without ceasing, but it is more blessed always to give thanks." We should love him but without expecting his love in return. This way we know we are not loving him out of fear. Love then becomes a creative act, one in which each day we are responsible for moving forward into a more perfect practice of self-forgetting.

He loves us by letting us take a very long time to make that practice perfect. Otherwise known as: grace. He lets us, and lets us in the freest free will, make mistakes and keep trying. The fact that I am still standing and have not yet been reduced to a smoking pile of ash is some proof that grace is his nature. If you need to take a long time to figure out whether you love him, he will not be impatient.

And maybe I won't be impatient. If you ever find yourself wandering forgetfully into a prayer, please pray for that. I can be too harsh. Harsher than God, which is pride. I was a little harsh in my last letter, and you were gracious enough not to remark upon it if you thought so.

What I think is that your fear is the problem here. Your fear, and the notion that you failed the Church because your sin eclipsed your love. (I'm relieved that you don't think the Church failed you because then you would be leaving a disgruntled customer, which would be a much harder position to dig out from. Resentment, and I should know, is a toxin that causes paralysis, if not eternal enmity.)

But I want you to think that perhaps you could be a knight of faith. You are the only person I have ever met who ever seemed capable of inhabiting and living up to Kierkegaard's term. I don't want to flatter you, but maybe you need a little bit of flattery right now.

Maybe you should leave off the Augustine and turn again to Kierkegaard and Dostoevsky. I know we've talked about these two a lot, but I want to repeat myself. The gospels tell us Christ suffered, but all we have as proof is the stained-glass triptych of Christ's suffering in Mark — the temptation in the desert, the praying in the garden of Gethsemane, crying out to God on the cross. It is helpful to know that Christ struggled with temptation — I am glad it is on the record — but sometimes it can feel like a bit of catechism we repeat without ever truly comprehending what he actually endured. But those two writers I think come closest to giving us the best modern articulation of what it means to struggle with what we have been charged with. They are poets of the agony that is doubt and of the burden that is conscience.

Bernard, I am about to flatter you again, but I think you could come up with an articulation that is as good as theirs. I think that if you wrote of this struggle, if you wrote of yourself, Bernard Eliot, born 1932, in Boston, Massachusetts, with all your very particular temptations and fears, and your craving for God's mercy, and the death that comes on from feeling so far from it, without glorifying yourself as a hero conquering this death but as someone in chains, it would be as powerful. I've said this to you before but I think you might need to hear it again. What I haven't told you before, because I thought your head was big enough without your hearing this, was that the first time I heard your poems, at the colony, I thought of John Donne. Perhaps you could look at his poems.

I think I have written enough, and maybe too much.

Love,
Frances

August 30, 1959

Frances, my favorite. If God exists, he exists only in you.

All my love,
Bernard

September 5, 1959

Dear Claire —

Thank you for having me last week. I was very glad that Old Man Sullivan let me out of his clutches long enough for me to escape to you and Bill. Please give Bill my love. I am very appreciative of how he smiles with us, and at us, and then drifts off to his work as if out of respect. And I am very appreciative of how he and I can sit and have coffee while you sleep and feel like friends too. He is also a whiz at finding delicious uses for the many sausages that populate Chicago. You are a very lucky woman, as I have said before.

I still feel a little ashamed of the way I refused to go on that hike when I saw the Doberman hanging around the entrance to the trail. Your car makes a nice place in which to nap. Bill was very nice about that too. Don't tell anyone. I try to make like I have steel intestines. I don't know what's gotten into me about dogs.

Could you send me the recipe for that pound cake you made for dessert on Saturday? Although I have a feeling mine will turn out to be a brick the first few times — you've always had a lighter touch than I when it comes to baking. I am convinced it is because you don't hold grudges.

Speaking of which. Thank you for listening to me talk about Bernard. But I reject your suggestion that I may be in love with him. When I try to conceive of who he is to me — and you know I never like to spend too much time brooding about what anyone other than family means to me, because that way lies disappointment and self-righteousness — I conceive of him as an older brother. I see him too clearly to be in love with him.

I maintain that the force of my feeling is familial — that whatever I feel for him is as protective and exasperated as what I feel for Ann, and perhaps even more intense, as it explodes with frequent awe of his brain. And with pain, when I think of his tired gray face, a face that was his but not his, steamrollered by drugs and exhaustion.

I cannot comprehend what he is going through. So my mother died when I was four — what real pain is that? I think my words and my presence offer no more solace to him than the solace offered a dog in petting his head. I'm just standing there, petting Bernard, ineffectually. Why should he want to hear from someone in, as it were, Rude Health? What could I have to say that would make any sense to him? And yet I wrote him, twice, imagining I did have something to say. I think I am starting to feel some guilt for the way I responded to him last spring. I rejected him, and yet he still calls me his favorite. He really must be crazy to do that.

Now I will confess I do think Bernard's handsome. You're Claire; I can't lie to you. He has physical vigor that appeals. He swims with an obliviously sloppy love of water, as if the ocean is a piece of paper he's ripping in half. I've seen him climb trees in the middle of a walk just to climb them, and I've seen him tear legs off steaming turkeys with no care for the heat because he could no longer wait to eat them. His brute force makes me laugh, and it makes me feel affection — affection — for him.

It was too hard, having seen this physical vigor, to see him as he was in the hospital.

I'm a little nervous at us being in close proximity when he starts teaching at Hunter College — Bernard is overwhelming even through the post — but am very glad he is returning to his usual routine.

What are you reading now? I am reading the Philip Roth you recommended. I don't know, Claire.

Roth makes me think of Ann. Of how she might get trapped. Sometimes when I listen to her, I think she's Yeats (prostration to an ideal despite its being a poison) and Maud Gonne (impervious to having done the poisoning) in one. It makes me want to slap her sometimes. Oh God. The older we get, the more I worry about her and her appetites. When I was younger they made me angry. She'd eat seconds when dinner was supposed to last us until next day's lunch, borrow my dresses without telling me, take money from my wallet (at least she'd leave a note, with apologetic exclamation marks, promising to pay me back) to go out with friends after she'd spent her own paycheck. You know all of this. Now they make me fear for her happiness. I fear that her pleasures will make her unhappy because she won't have work that will keep her from boredom, because her inability to see the emptiness of beauty will lead her to choose poorly when she chooses a husband. My father indulged her — he was the younger of two, the second to a studious favored older brother, and I think he let my sister do as she liked because, even as he favored me for my studiousness, he knew that he was doing to her what had been done to him. Whenever I complained about some unpunished scam of hers, my father always said her sins were harmless ones, and asked me to try not to be so upset with her — and this was from a man who never made demands of anybody. Still, Ann thinks I'm my father's favorite, and I keep silent when she goes down that road. I know that I am. I'm his favorite because I'm the priest, studious and abstemious, that his brother never became. He loves Ann with ferocity, though. Through spoiling and flirting and tossing her rotters off of the porch. He loves me like a son and Ann like a daughter. And I have taken care of both of them like a mother. I don't mean to sound bitter there. I'm not.

I don't know why exactly I went on like this. You know all this.

Ann's been on my mind. I have just invited her to come visit me — can you believe she has never come to visit me in New York? I think she's jealous that she isn't here too. Or maybe she has stayed away from some sort of spite. We don't say this to each other, but we have a silent pact: I took care of my father for years, and now Ann must stay behind and do it. For at least a little while. Anyway, I've invited her to come visit, and I think I worry about us having a good enough time. Although I know this isn't about me having a good time. I want her to have a good time.

Claire, these thoughts are exactly the ones that will keep me from having a family. When I think of what family is I can see only boredom, chronic misunderstanding, loss, bickering, abuse, burdens that are borne out of duty but never bear love as their fruit. I'm sorry — you know I don't mean that I don't understand why you and Bill might want to have one. You know I am talking purely of my own jaundiced stance.

Well, I should go now. Look at all I've written. I should get to bed. Thank you again for my visit.

Love,
Frances

September 13, 1959

Dear Claire —

I am sending you a book that we are publishing that for once I am not disgusted by. Have you heard of this woman? This is her second novel; I'd never heard of her. It's about a group of older women living out their last days in a London boarding house during the war. This novel is short, about two hundred pages, and there is authority in the writer's conviction that she knows her characters well enough, and can draw them well enough, that she doesn't need to go on that long to get what she needs out of them. But perhaps this spoke to me purely because of having lived at the henhouse.

Ann came to visit. I think she enjoyed herself. She met me at the office for lunch one day, and I introduced her to everyone. "You two are sisters?" said Old Man Sullivan. Peter, whom I think I've told you about, said the same thing. By which they meant: *Why aren't you that pretty, Frances?* "Frances is such a good cook," Ann responded both times. I think she was trying to advertise that I had a dowry too. I heard one young editor whistle appreciatively when we left the office he shares with a few other boys. Then at lunch we found her a dress at Bonwit Teller. I pitched in a few dollars. But the differences between us give me a kind of heart attack whenever they present themselves. Sample anecdotes: We are walking along Central Park West, on our way to the park. My sister sees an actor from a television show. "Oh, it's X," she says, clutching my arm. "Oh," I say, and keep walking. "No, no, I'm going to get an autograph." "Oh no you're not," I say. "Why not?" Ann says. "Aunt Peggy and Aunt Helen would think it's a hoot." I say: "It's groveling for something that's not even admirable to begin with!" "Oh, stop it," Ann says. "Come with me." "No!" I say. I take my arm away from her hand and stop walking. I turn into the seven-year-old I think she's being. "You're such a sourpuss," she says, and strides off to this actor and the woman he's with. I can't even watch. When she comes back she's waving the receipt from the grocery store we stopped in. It has his autograph. "See! He was very nice," she says. "He has family in Philadelphia." She says this like it means something, like she has really made a connection with him. It's like being with an old woman who still believes in Santa Claus. Next street anecdote: We go take a walk after dinner to get ice cream and we are about to pass a very old couple, probably in their eighties, both short, frail, the man in a short-sleeved pressed shirt and slacks, very neat, glasses, and he is pushing his wife, in a short-sleeved dress with huge flowers on it, in a wheelchair. Since the street we're on has a bit of an incline, Ann thinks we should offer our help. He doesn't look as if he is wrestling with the incline, and still she says to me, "Oh, do you think we should offer to help?" "Oh, I don't know," I say, shy, because perhaps they will think us young people patronizing, because perhaps they will resent our pity of their age and fragility. But Ann says to them, brightly, a chipmunk in a blue-checked dress, "Do you need help?" "No," says the man, without interest, but with no frost either. And so I'm proved right. And I wish I hadn't been. I see Ann: willing to insert herself into the world to help, unafraid of how it will be received, just knowing that as a Catholic she must be kind, and me hanging back, afraid of being seen as smug in my small offer of help when everyone needs so much help all the time, the amount of help needed is too big, and so I turn away in despair. *Keep yourself hid, Ann,* I am always saying to her, and *Frances, you are a miser,* she is always saying to me. It's like liturgy. But unlike liturgy, no change comes about from repeating the phrases. There's comfort in it, but no change.

She also told me that she is seeing someone. She didn't say much about him — by now Ann knows that I will probably disapprove of whomever she is seeing. I should feel bad about that but I like to think that it will do some good one day. His name is Michael, and she met him, she said, at the engagement party of one of the girls from work. She said he's going to school for surveying at night and working as a manager at the Acme during the day. He's another Italian. Ann likes Italians. My aunts tease her about it. They're so warm, she says. They're such warm people.

I should get this in the mail. Bernard is coming for dinner and has hinted that he wants me to bake him something; meanwhile, it's four p.m. and I am still in a nightdress.

Love,
Frances

September 14, 1959

Dear Frances —

Now that we live in the same city, I guess we won't be writing to each other anymore. But I wanted to send you a note after seeing you last night. Thank you for making me dinner. I don't know what you were talking about with that pound cake — there was absolutely no way that a kitten tied to it and thrown in a river would sink to the bottom instantly. I can't cook at all, and I am starting to see the wisdom of the henhouse — three squares for the feckless. If I were any more shameless, I would ask if I could come to dinner once a week. You could think of yourself as the Red Cross. Christian Aid. The YMCA. I would pay for the groceries.

See, we can keep up a conversation without God at the center: Roth, Updike, my students, your coworkers, your work, my work, your father, my mother, your landlord. I mean to keep you in my life. And I see that you don't want me leaving either. I see how you smile when I am around — your lips purse, and then they tilt to the left, like a boat lifted by the swell of a wave.

I am glad that you let me sit at your table again. And that you let me toast your beautiful, fearsome book.

Love,
Bernard

February 20, 1960

Dear Claire —

I can't thank you enough for coming to New York. John Percy thought you were fantastic, and Bernard did too. "Claire," he said, "has Pre-Raphaelite vapors curling around her Katharine Hepburn angles."

Thank you for coming to that dinner. I always feel like I need to keep the drool off the front of my dress around John. He still makes me nervous, even though I make him laugh, but I think that's good. Thank you for charming Sullivan too, Claire. I'm sure you stupefied him with your Pre-Raphaelite vapors. And I'm sure Bernard would have been twice as drunk if you hadn't been there. And would have given a speech that was three times, not just two times, the length of John's. (Bernard. I have to admit, his testimony on my behalf made me blush, and if he had not been at that table I would have experienced a great sadness. Although I was glad John finally cut him off.) As you know, I am not the world's best celebrant. I hope I appeared grateful. I was grateful. But I don't know how to bring off being the center of attention or how to accept the mantle of honored guest. I will take a Pulitzer through the mail, however. That is fine. But I kept wanting to get up and clear the table.

I went home last weekend for a visit and my sister told anyone who would listen: "Frances has just published a novel!" At church, on the street, in the grocery store. More inability to gracefully accept being the center of attention. But then also annoyed by others' inability to gracefully accept my being the center of attention! "Oh, I've written a book," says a woman, middle-aged, white acrylic cardigan, handbag on arm, standing out on the steps after Mass. And then, of course, it turns out it's St. Aloysius's parish cookbook. And from someone else: "Oh, my brother's written a book" — a six-hundred-page novel retelling their family's flight out of Ireland that he has refused to send to publishers. Next: "Oh, I've written a book" — a handbook for CCD teachers. People refuse to be simply impressed or to express congratulations. It's as if they feel threatened by something that is arguably more real than their efforts, or perhaps they are embarrassed by not knowing what to ask an Artist — and I'm not even saying that I am one! — so they turn the conversation back to themselves. And/or they are narcissists. I would never say to someone who paints, *Oh, I enjoy taking an easel to the park,* or say to a surgeon, *Oh, in high school I could dissect an infant pig in thirty seconds flat.* Look, I would rather people not know what I've done in the first place. Indifference would be better.

And when people tell me they've bought a copy — people who know my father and Ann tangentially, people who have only *Reader's Digest* in the house — I'm mortified. Why have they done this for me, a stranger? If Bill's sister wrote a book, I don't think I'd buy it. No offense. And these people will be mystified and horrified when they actually open it. They're going to wonder if they've accidentally bought something that's on the Index of Forbidden Books.

My aunts, of course, are making a concerted effort to behave as if I've done nothing at all — at home they embraced me briskly and asked pointedly about my job. Fine by me. I would rather not talk about it with them either. Ann gave my aunt Helen a copy — which I told her not to do, but Ann is a pushover, and my aunt Helen is a manipulator — and Helen told Ann she could not finish the book because she was so upset by how mean I was being to the nuns. I think Peggy and Mary and Helen have always wondered what I really believe, and now, based on the testimony of my aunt Helen, they will suspect that they've been raising an infidel all this time. They will cluck and sigh for my soul among themselves. They don't know what to do with a book about God that does not stink of piety the way Thérèse of Lisieux stank of roses. They would not be able to see that the nuns brought their calamities unto themselves, and that we are always and everywhere, every single one of us, as sinful as those nuns. They will feel only persecuted because it will seem that I am persecuting the thing that they have been taught never to question.

Thank God for my father. "Sister John is Sister Anne, isn't she?" We were out on a walk after dinner. Yes, I said. "And Sisters Monica and Barbara are your aunt Mary and uncle Tom." Yes, I said. He laughed. And then he said: "They'll never know." And laughed again.

Some reviews are in — *Time* decided they didn't hate it enough to fully trounce it, but the reviewer seemed subconsciously disappointed that it was not a different book entirely, and since he did not realize the nature of his disappointment, he could not write a review that exposed the book's true flaws and strengths. His review just exposed his wish not to be reading a novel about a bunch of nuns.

The Old Testament metaphors are coming fast and thick. Someone else said that I "wielded prose like Judith, head of Holofernes triumphantly in hand." Lord. And yet another person wrote approvingly that the book "throbbed with the kind of wicked wisdom deployed by King Solomon when, in the book of 1 Kings, two women came to him, each claiming to be the mother of a baby boy, and he declared that the only thing to be done was to cut the boy in half." Am I a Hun and just don't know it?

Am I from Pittsburgh and just don't know it? Someone else misidentified my city of birth as Pittsburgh.

In my actual city of birth, the *Inquirer* declared that "Miss Reardon has a disturbingly tidy sense of justice that is, even as it disturbs, piquant." Why, thank you.

Re the *Times:* I'm relieved.

Thank you again.

Love,
Frances

March 12, 1960

Ted —

Thank you, as always, for the visit. I'm sorry you had to leave early on Saturday because of that deposition. You always say lawyers give lousy parties, and we could have taken you to the party for this new journal Carl is putting out. The party was a hydra-headed rugby scrum of all the usual suspects, but no less entertaining because of it.

Do you remember Betsy, that friend of Caroline who sipped at only one Manhattan that long night we went out for Caroline's graduation? She had been seeing a young man I introduced her to, Robert, a graduate student in philosophy who sat in on one of my classes. He took to me because, I think, he does not have a father and his older brothers are far-flung and all in the armed services. He came to my office one day a couple of weeks ago asking for some advice and so we got a drink. He told me a story: He was helping to teach a philosophy course presided over by a professor emeritus and while he'd been sitting there, tending the wan fire that was the old man's drone, tossing in a spark of clarification here and there whenever the flames threatened to go out for good, he noticed this girl sitting in the middle distance of the lecture hall, red hair wound back in a bun, with a placid, impassive, and sometimes dismissive expression that flared up in a way that made Robert start to have ideas about her own fire, and then afterward she asked him for advice on a paper, and so they went to a café and they ended up talking for a few hours, and the girl told him her whole life story: doubly orphaned by polio, lost at Hunter. He finds himself wanting to touch this girl as she talks, finds himself alive — my paraphrasing, because Robert was too removed from his own appetites to know what he was succumbing to — finds himself alive to beauty with the idea that beauty noticed must be beauty consumed (which I don't think he has followed to its logical conclusion, because if he had, he wouldn't be as alive to it in this momentarily problematic way). He knows, however, that he loves Betsy. But the redhead doesn't know that, because Robert hasn't had the heart to bring it up.

So he reaches out and takes this girl's hand over the table, and, wouldn't you know it, Betsy has taken off work early to surprise him with a visit. Alas, *she* gets the surprise when she sees them in the window in the café on her way to the office — sees them just at the moment Robert reached for this girl's hand — and she reacts as if Robert's Don José and this girl's Carmen, and she leaves and calls him up and breaks it off. She hasn't been, Robert told me, with very many men, and so, he suspects, she was acting in the way she'd heard you should when you find a leak in the boat, without even bothering to determine how big the leak is. I felt pity for Robert when we talked. His anxious eyes behind his glasses — it was like looking through the cracked windowpanes of a looted store, as if someone had broken in and robbed him of any sense, and I could hear the shattered glass still tinkling on the recently stampeded floor of his brain. Betsy knew no other response to this scene but to prosecute and deport, and he knew no other response to her response but to become a hermit in a cave of guilt. "Have neither of you ever heard of the word *peccadillo*?" I said to him. I'd be attracted to Betsy too, I think, except that she is too wilting a stem for me. Betsy is a girl who is receptive, passive, the kind of girl who sang madrigals in college because it allowed her to gambol in a field that had not yet been carpeted over with the weeds of Weltschmerz, and who will marry in order to build herself a castle against the invasion of Weltschmerz, children her moat, husband her drawbridge. There is a sweetness she was trying to overcompensate for by prosecuting Robert. And with him, shame overtook his passion for Betsy. Someone needed to get these two talking to each other because they were both too committed to their own righteousness, both twenty-four years old and not out of the nursery quite yet.

So I invited Betsy to this party, and then I invited Robert, assuring them both that I had not invited the other, assuring them both that I knew for a fact that the other would not be there because they'd each told me they had plans. And there they were. I stood in a corner and watched. I pulled Frances over too and she claimed she didn't want any part of this, but I held her by the arm and anchored her to the spot, and she stayed and watched as the two of them stared at each other like stunned deer. "She's going to bolt first," said Frances, and Betsy did, but Robert reached out for her arm to make her stay (here Frances pulled away from my own grip) and Betsy began crying — crying! — and Robert took her into his arms. "Don't think you have a talent for this sort of thing," said Frances as we walked away to get another cocktail. I am very pleased, and, yes, more than a little proud, and Robert tells me all has been forgiven. Including me for my Prospero-esque conjuring. I can't stand for people to be weak-willed and stiff-necked on principle.

But this was what I meant to tell you. Frances was really very pleased to see you and was really very touched by your taking us to the Oak Room in her book's honor. (What she won't tell you is that when you and I came back from the men's room, I saw her slipping a cocktail stirrer into her purse.) I know you told me that if I confessed to her what I confessed to you, she would never talk to me again, but Ted, I am starting to feel that she may eventually be receptive. That night I had the extreme pleasure of watching Frances betray what I thought just might be one filament of jealousy. At the party there was a girl who interviewed me for the *Paris Review* last year. A black-haired girl, rounded and tall like a caryatid, a little too stiff and erect as well, with something suggesting she'd be quite comfortable shouldering greatness, something suggesting she could see from your present into your future and then into your past and back again, each eye a steady, blank forbidding lake — but an expansive air about her when she gets talking, and during the interview we'd debated for some time about the merits of E. M. Forster. I couldn't see it, because, having actually loved Christ, having spent so much time on the sea with Ulysses, it is very hard for me to view Bloomsbury as anything more than an incestuous séance cocooned in an anti-Victorian Victorianism that makes me cede greatness to your actually eminent Victorians, though by the end of the interview she made me understand that at the very least I might prefer Forster to Woolf. She introduced herself to me again at the party and I thanked her for her piece. She asked me what I had been reading lately and I told her.

I had not detected anything flirtatious in her manner, but then Frances came by while we were talking about Philip Larkin (I envy his control, but it's the kind of envy that transpires when you recognize your own fundamental inability to become the thing you envy, which then leaves you to settle freely into unqualified respect). The girl, I thought, stiffened, I suppose because Frances had arrived and was standing there in a silence of aplomb that suggested she and I shared daily proximity. I then took Frances by the hand and said, "This is Frances Reardon. She's just written a beautiful novel." "I've heard about your book," said the girl, leveling a gaze at Frances and then issuing a very perfunctory "Congratulations." "You've got nothing to worry about," said Frances. "He's not mine." "I'm not worried at all," said the girl. Although she did look a little taken aback. "I'm going to leave you two," said Frances, and then she did. It was very hard not to laugh. Sometimes I wish women would just go ahead and throw the punch. If that were the case, I'd bet every time on Frances.

Yours,
Bernard

April 5, 1960

Dear Frances —

I want to write this so you know that I've thought this over and am telling you what I feel in a slightly cooler moment. I would call you but I fear you would hang up on me. Or that you might not pick up at all.

I'm writing this between classes. It's 10:30. A student just floated his head in the window pleadingly but I waved him off. I hear collegial repartee and purposeful footsteps outside the door. I see Lexington Avenue below me through the window to my right. I see all the children still in their winter coats crossing and recrossing the street in a pattern that makes me think of the hedges in gardens in Florence.

I am not sorry that I kissed you. Again. So now I will tell you that I want you in an unseemly, criminal, animal way.

I speak to make myself clear. I speak, admittedly, to stir you, if there is something in you to be stirred.

You will think I'm going mad again. I know I'm not. If I were mad, this would be rhyming.

Call me when you get this letter.

Bernard

June 1, 1960

Dear Claire —

Please forgive me for not having replied to your past two letters.

Bernard and I have been engaging in what might in a court of law be called an affair. I have seen him many nights for many weeks. I have slept in his bed. Claire, this person has gotten me into his bed. In a nightgown, I assure you, but into his bed. He says that he is in love with me. I believe that he thinks he is. He may actually be. I have not told him that I am in love with him. Because I don't know what I think. He says he does not mind this. He knows me, he says, and he knows that I need to get my mind around it before I start making pronouncements. He is right. But I am scared. I am scared even to describe to you what it has felt like, the enjoyment I take in being described as something beautiful. That's right: he calls me beautiful. I want to laugh myself sometimes when he says it.

I don't know if I love him, but I do know that I love being called beautiful by Bernard. This is a confusion. I feel shame. I think I now need to be easier on my sister. I could never tell Ann about this or ask her advice. It would be like asking an alcoholic how to get off the sauce.

I don't think that there's sin here. That's not it. Not even in forgetting — perhaps forgiving — that he says he does not believe. The sin will come because I sin against Bernard's hopes. Or if I get hopes and then he sins against them. For my part, I am determined to not have hopes. I would rather be sinned against than sinning. I could not bear to hurt him. I feel like I am the only one who can know the truth about what is happening between us, and it's up to me to be on the lookout for any signs of his tiring, or his illness. Do you remember that night after we gave that party and, because Ed was genially drunk, we insisted on his staying? And then you went to bed and he insisted, genially, on kissing me, and I found that I could not refuse him? I knew he was kissing me because he was upset about losing out on the fellowship and confused about Ellen's demands and wanted comfort and power the only way he was used to getting it away from the typewriter: from women. It was like giving blood to the Red Cross — I let him draw what he needed from me while I waited patiently, unmoved, for it to be over, and after he left I went to the kitchen and ate a doughnut.

There's some of that here.

I find I can't say much more than this about it to you. And you are my truest friend. I'm afraid I might offend you, or annoy you and burden you with the dramatic irony of my confessions. (I said one thing, but you, Claire, knew all along that it was just the opposite. This has already happened — I wrote you a letter a while back saying that I was not in love with him. And now look.)

I am just as idiotic about human love as the nuns who raised me. A normal woman would know what to feel and why she was feeling what she felt, or she'd just say, To hell with feelings, I'll take the money and run. I don't know how these things work, and this is making me panic some. There's a part of me that thinks Bernard just might get tired of me and, come September, when he has to start teaching, pack his desire for me away. You hear about these things. I know that he is not like that, that he has to have the girl remove herself or be forcibly removed from the girl, but I do worry that I am a mirage in the middle of some spree, and this makes me hesitant.

Please advise.

Love,
Frances

June 10, 1960

F —

For God's sake! First: He's in love with you! Let's put that question to rest. I saw the way he looked at you the night we went out to celebrate your book. Like a dog that's spent one minute too long on a chain. He also looked high — and that was long before we all got hammered. He looked like an amusing bit of mess — a mess *you* made. Repeat after me: *Bernard is in love with Frances.*

Second: Do take enjoyment in being called beautiful. We'll all be wizened apples soon enough.

Third: Please try to enjoy his attentions. Look, you're absolutely right to worry about his mental health. I'm not saying that you should bury your head in the sand on that point. But maybe I am saying that you should let him ravish you. You've spent too long looking at men suspiciously. Which is not to say they don't deserve it. But you are in New York City and you are a young woman who has published her first of many books, and to great success! This isn't *The Best of Everything* — you're not going to end up dead in an Upper East Side stairwell because you didn't know how to take no for an answer. Bernard is in no way like Ed, whose lovemaking you had to supplement with a doughnut. Look at Bernard like a complimentary dish of baked Alaska brought to you by a fine and appreciative dining establishment — something you didn't know you wanted but now that it's being served up to you, you find it's impossible to resist. I don't really think you know how handsome he is. I'd feel lucky enough just getting to walk in someplace and make an entrance with that man, never mind have his hands on me. In the early days of a love affair, a lady should be carefree, even greedy. These days are the best part. They are what you will have to rely on to make you fall in love with your beloved again later, when the fire's gone out — and you're already wasting them on worry. Please don't sabotage this before it's begun. You're at the last stanza of Keats's ode — Cold Pastoral — when you should be lolling around at the first — Wild Ecstasy. You only think you know what you can't handle.

This is how these things work.

I don't know what will happen between you two. I don't even know yet what I think *should* happen between the two of you. I might write you another letter tomorrow telling you to stay away from him. But if we all ran away from what scared us — I'm not even sure how to end that sentence, though I think we could both come up with about a dozen answers that would send you running toward what scared you, as a point of human pride.

You are to write me anytime about this. You and I have only each other to rely on in these matters, not being normal women.

Love,
Claire

June 30, 1960

Dear Claire —

Thank you. You not only gave me advice but made me laugh, and I needed that, maybe as much as I needed advice. What you say makes sense. I will try to, per William James, act *as if* — *as if* Bernard is true.

Love,
Frances

July 10, 1960

Dearest Frances —

I wish you had come up here to Maine with me to visit Ted. He says hello. "That girl," he says, "is a serious girl. That girl will take a bad joke, look at you with pity, and then make a much better one out of it." I think he is jealous of me. As he should be. A man always wants his friends to be a little in love with his beloved too.

There is a large bed here, right under a window, framed in pine branches, summer's frost, from which I can see the sea, and in the mornings I think of what your bare arms, covered in freckles, would look like in the clear bright water. In the afternoons I wonder whether the salt water heated by the sun would stain your skin and leave behind a reticulation — an Irish articulation of Venusian sea foam. Your freckles: I want to down them like oysters, having my fill on a rock that no one can find.

I've been up here thinking of your breasts and masturbating like a weed of a boy who's been told it could get rid of his acne. Why did you have to be virtuous and stay in the city? I would have allowed you your own room. And there would be enough people here to make a buffer between you and my avarice. These are good solid people Ted has collected from law school, and there's also a screenwriter who fled Hollywood for newspaper reporting in Boston, and so when swimming is finished and debate about the election has waned, the screenwriter can serve up gossip about who is an alcoholic and who is secretly seeing whom. Which means there are no women here to pry into what you mean to me. Ted's wife is too busy organizing a DAR luncheon to care. (I wish I were joking.) Plus, there are real oysters here that we have been downing like shots in some vinegar.

I am tempted to write a whole letter full of things that will make you blush. I am tempted to write indecent things that will make you angry. But I have the soul of a Puritan and this prevents me from letting my desires billow out in a more baroque, black-velveted, Sade-ian manner. Correction, and how could I have made that mistake: A Puritan would be content to love an absence. I am not. I can say only this very artless, sweet-hearted thing, which is that you are velvet-skinned and freckled, and I will not be able to sleep tonight because of it.

Your
Bernard

July 11, 1960

My love.

I'm up and looking at the moon on the ocean and I'm thinking.

The air around you is sometimes wary and chill. I think you are waiting for me to become bored with you. I think you think I have gone out of my mind a little, maybe. Please believe that I love you.

There's nothing I can say to convince you. I know whatever I say will sound like ravings. Love letters are allowed to sound like ravings, but when you have a history of raving, that pass is revoked. I can imagine how I sounded in the letter I just sent you. But it's a pleasure for me to sing to you. And to not care that it may sound like Mozart — a ridiculous fecundity of notes, and a sweetness therein. I know you hate Mozart.

I have many things to sing of because I have a friend I can call beautiful. I have always thought you were beautiful — I was stunned by your blue eyes at lunch at the colony that day, your eyes widening, laughing, listening, suspicious, fixed on me and never wandering, and I remember thinking, *What a pretty neck that girl has, her arms and neck have curves that portend more alluring curves below; how open and speckled her face is, like a day lily.* And everyone else there desiccated by drink, ambition, and fear. I know, that's cruel. I'm a little desiccated by drink myself. You had the radiance of someone who knew her worth and would not squander it. You did not rob anyone to feel that worth, I could tell. You came by it at birth. Like I did. But by the end of that lunch I think your final aloofness — a consequence of knowing your worth — must have put all those thoughts in the deep freeze, or maybe it was something you said about Aquinas that had me filing you away as a classmate for catechism. Actually, maybe it was what you said about Mozart — that it sounded like damn tittering, and you preferred Bach, because it was cavernous and blackened with the soot of burned incense. And there was Lorraine, like Salome, bracelets jangling out a signal that meant she was at loose ends, slippery, available, ephemeral. What did I hear when I sat next to you? A breeze, and then heavy silence. A breeze, and then heavy silence. A sound I could wind my watch by. Self-possession, both intellectual and spiritual, and a merriness tempered by a predilection to judge. I liked it. But after all my panting for ideal love, I was in the mood for a divertimento.

Having spent hours looking at you, hours touching you, I know the many ways in which you are beautiful. But you were my friend first — not an idea about art or Tolstoy or purity or blond hair — and I think you are my friend still. I may not believe in God but I do believe that Simone Weil is right when she commands us to see people as they are and not turn them into creatures of our imagination. I am trying to look at you with love but without illusions.

I love your suspicion — it means that your mind is always sharpening itself against the many lies of this world — but right now it is killing me. So I am going to ask you to write me a letter convincing me that you believe me. You do not have to tell me that you are in love with me, and you do not have to tell me how you feel about me. You have to write and tell me that you believe I love you.

Your
Bernard

July 13, 1960

Dear Miss Reardon —

This is Ted. How is New York? Maine has been swell. Did you not want to come because you were not sure you could get yourself to a Mass in Maine? Have you not heard that there are French Canadians, and their attendant papistry, all over the place up here?

Let me begin by saying that Bernard has not put me up to this letter. I have never before intervened in a romance, but he's like a brother to me, and I like you a whole lot, and he said something the other day that made me think you needed some assurance as to the truth of his feelings. I know what Bernard is like when he is not in his right mind. This is not that. I have seen him through many infatuations. This is not that. How do I know? He talked about those girls all the time. They weren't returning his affection, so he had to talk about them to make them real. He had to do all the work, and this made him surly. He picked fights with me, with people at bars. With you — no talk, surliness, no fights. He keeps to himself about it. He seems calm. It's like he knows being calm is what you need to see how deep, solid, true, and stupid his love for you is. I almost tripped over him coming back from the beach the other day — he was asleep on the lawn, and he had your book spread over his chest, one arm flung out to the side like a flag and he was the snoring, quaking pole. The look on his face was one of complete peace. I thought: He's far gone. Rest assured that I'm telling you the truth. We lawyers don't believe in perjury.

Affectionately,
Ted

July 15, 1960

Bernard —

You're right — I don't know what to believe. I'm sorry that my suspicion is killing you. I know what I want to believe, which is that you are not in the grip of an infatuation. I want to believe that. Very much. I will try to stop giving you a chill and wary air.

The Hudson River says hello. It doesn't know what you see in New England's blustering surf. It thinks a body of water earns its majesty by knowing how to keep its own counsel. That said, it is very secretly envious of something so effusive.

Love,
Frances

July 15, 1960

Dear Ted —

Thank you for writing what you did. I appreciate that you were looking out for your friend. I wrote Bernard the day I received your letter.

I'd send a peach pie through the mail but I trust only Jersey peaches and it looks like they don't let them into the city.

I hope to see you again soon.

Affection returned,
Frances

July 20, 1960

Frances —

My love. You are sly, you are charming, you are never going to do what I ask in the way I want you to, but that is charming too, and I will see you in four days, which is far too far away.

Bernard

July 30, 1960

Dear Claire —

Congratulations on getting that job at the *Tribune*! I'm sure after you've spent a year on their women's pages they'll have you trailing the cops on the South Side. That boss of yours sounds hilarious. Like a big camellia with the teeth of a Venus flytrap in a vase of gabardine and with a bosom of granite. I think I just wrote a Picasso painting. "Your copy or your hide!" That would get me writing. After I stopped laughing. And she plays tennis too with that bosom? This confirms my idea about management: The competitively sporty excel. They like games; they have stamina. And you need stamina to put up with the games played by those above and below you. You played tennis too — you'll be fine. But I like to swim.

You ask me how I am feeling. I find that it is very, very hard for me to put into words what I am feeling. I know you will forgive me for being Frances. I hope Bernard forgives me for being Frances. He seems to not mind that I do not articulate my affection very often. He knows, for example, to kiss me out on the street and not in a roomful of people. He shows so much affection to me, I think he sometimes does not notice my inability to show it. Sometimes. "Frances," he said the other night after dinner, "often I think the only real evidence of your love is the amount you cook for me." He was right. I make him bread. I make him cakes. Pies. And it's summer. I am behaving the way I behave at home: standoffishly, and pies to offset the standoff-ishness. The bread and pies are beads on a rosary, paces to go through because I can't think how I might love of my own accord.

I am hoping that God will forgive me for being Frances.

I will try to put two feelings into words. First, when I am walking down the street to meet him and I know that I have come into his view, and his eyes, as I approach, are giving off sparks of both hunger and affection, the two fighting it out like cats in his pupils, I feel that I would do anything to have that look cast upon me for the rest of my days. I feel that I am known more intimately than perhaps God knows me. And now I have blasphemed, so please burn this letter.

Second, do you remember when we sat in that booth at McKellan's with Bob and Roger, and Roger looked at me and said: "I bet when you finally find someone who sends you, he'll be Mrs. O'Leary's cow and you'll be Chicago"? For many years now, as you know, my official position on this assessment was to be offended. Who did Roger presume to be, making pronouncements on my womanhood — and without the excuse of flirtation, because he was courting you? Well, now I know what Roger was on about. I thank him for his prescience. Otherwise I might have mistakenly taken myself to the doctor.

Claire! I can't even say what I mean to you.

Here is one more feeling. Sometimes I look at him, searching for signs that his illness is about to erupt. Sometimes I think I see it about his face. About his apartment. Dishevelment; neglect; impassioned responses to small daily events, from a piece in the *Times* that seems to be vaguely conceding to the right wing, to whatever I am up to in the kitchen, to a student paper filled with exceptional insights. A mountain of dishes in the sink, cigarette butts floating in a pan. His dress shirts stuffed in the linen closet with worn bath towels — I am surprised he even has bath towels and does not dry himself off with newspaper. (He says Ted's mother gave them to him out of alarm.) No shower curtain. Papers all over his bed; when he's not sleeping in it, his bed is a credenza, with a dozen different mugs and whiskey tumblers beside it. He cut his foot a couple of weeks ago because he was hung over and forgot to steer clear of them when getting out of bed. He will call four separate times at work; I can't answer it the first three times, and the fourth time, when I pick up, he'll say: "Why didn't you pick up before? You're Florence Nightingale, you're supposed to pick up. I could be bleeding on a field in Turkey." We laugh, it's funny, but the fact remains: He has called four times in a row in the span of five minutes. "I wanted to hear your voice in the middle of this day," he'll say. Or: "What's the soonest possible hour we can meet this evening?" Or: "If I had to assign a poem from Hopkins today, what poem should it be?" It makes me want to hide from him sometimes in embarrassment — I have maybe a tenth of his energy, and I often wonder when he will realize that he's in love with a slug. Whirlwinds can't love slugs. They need other whirlwinds, don't they? Or mountains.

When I was about six or seven I was convinced that my father would pass away suddenly because my mother needed him with her in what I guess I was calling heaven — I would wake up thinking, *Today might be the day, and then we will have to go live with our aunts.* It was a pain I woke up with many mornings. I had forgotten that I used to feel this way, but I'm feeling something like this now. I wake up every morning with an obscure worry that eventually takes the shape of this sentence: *Is today the day that Bernard will disappear?* Each morning I wake to think the view I see outside is a sign of storm: leaves flipped over to show their dull underside, shoved there by a wind tugging thunder and rain behind it. And then I dress and find myself on the street, in the sunshine, and I make my way to the subway, and the sun and the crowds soak up my worry.

I wrote this at work. I should now get back to writing my story.

My love to you —
Frances

August 15, 1960

Ted —

I envy you, still up in Maine. I'm writing you from the colony. Which is perfectly fine, but no Ted, no ocean, no lobster. I called them up last week to see if they could give me two weeks here, because I want to get a head start on this next book before I begin teaching, and they said, "Be our guest." So I'll be spending the last two weeks of the summer here, and then back to New York, and then classes begin.

I wish you had come with me to Philadelphia to visit Frances's people (that is what she calls them, her people) because I think they are like your people — boisterous, welcoming — only without money. I would have liked to see you tell these people they don't deserve pensions.

Just how did I get there? It began this way. "My aunts want to meet you," said Frances a few weeks ago. "I have had a phone call. They are commanding me to bring you home, because my father is too gentlemanly to make the request. Are you ready to be smothered by the loudest hospitality north of the Mason-Dixon?"

She wasn't kidding. The women, her mother's sisters and their daughters, all laugh in the same key — they throw their heads back and rasp out nine notes in rapid succession, nine eighth notes spilling down the scale. And they laugh quite a lot. They turn ruddy and have to fan themselves with their hands while wheezing out the last bits of laughter. They like to make one another laugh, but no one steps over anyone's joke to do so. Frances does not laugh, but she likes to make them laugh. I saw her sitting back, watching, eyes dancing, waiting for her chance to nonchalantly offer up the one thing that would set everyone off again, waiting in a supreme confidence that what she was about to say would of course set everyone off again — a polo player swooping in on his horse at the last moment to give the ball the winning crack.

Her father laughs too, but he laughs mostly with his eyes — I think he has given this to Frances. Where her aunts will use jokes to tell stories, he'll tease you. Though he won't tease Ann, her sister, I've noticed, who is quite beautiful. Long, strawberry-blond hair, big blue eyes like Frances's, slender, though plump in the necessary places, limbs rounded and smooth — comely fruit in a basket. When they stand side by side, in silence, you cannot see where they are sisters, their coloring and dress are so different. One is as resplendent (pink-and-white shoes intricately tooled, clusters of pearls in the ears, that strawberry-blond hair as proudly displayed and arranged about the shoulders as an ermine cape, all of it suggesting a child's delight in hoarding treasure) as the other is pin-tucked (chaste fabrics suitable for nightgowns; a face authoritative but shy, sheltering itself under reddish-brown bangs; feet shod in ladylike, unremarkable shoes; no jewelry but her eyes). It's like Helen of Troy next to Joan of Arc. Ann's prettiness makes her a cartoon — it makes Frances disappear for a little while — she is so emphatically a confection that it turns her into a cipher, and she may be complicit in that. She has a sense of humor, but that is overtaken by a sense of propriety. "Daddy!" Ann said in a hissing whisper like a switch on his behind when her father said, upon meeting me: "Where did you think you were going to hide him, Frances? He's as tall as Lincoln." And Frances standing next to me, smiling, smiling, smiling — a playwright standing in the wings, thrilled by her characters complying for the hundredth time.

But then when she and Ann start talking and laughing together, there's an eerily identical duet of inflections and motions that wake their faces up into resemblance. "You and your sister may be more alike than you admit," I said to her later. "Oh," she said. "That part's no different from being in a family band — we can harmonize at the drop of a hat, but I will go to my grave shaking my head over her."

A victory, one of several that day: A girl of about five, a daughter of one of the cousins, whose names I could not keep straight, asked if she could touch my hair. I lifted her up and said, "Go ahead," which gave her great pleasure. And myself, I have to admit. I can understand why certain dogs let certain children dress them in baby bonnets. She stared at me, mesmerized, grabbing two fistfuls of brush where my horns might be, scrunching her nose up to denote how serious and scientific this application of force was. Those blue, blue eyes again! I was starting to think that I had stumbled into a Celtic folktale that was going to end with one of these blue-eyed sorceresses turning me into a tree. "Kitty!" a woman said, calling out from across the crowded living room. That row home was so packed and electric with people of various ages, voices, and purposes — talking, cooking, drink-fixing, nut-eating, sport-betting, child-minding, dog-petting — it was like Washington Square on a Saturday afternoon. "Stop messing with Frances's friend's hair! You'll hurt him!" Frances came and took the girl off me. "Come on, Kitty," she said. "That man has nice hair," said Kitty as she sailed down to the ground. "Yes, he does," I heard Frances say, her back to me, before giving Kitty a kiss and sending her off into the crowd. I gloated to myself. Now if I could only get her to say those things to my face.

While sitting on the couch next to Ann, discussing baseball, thinking that I'd shown myself to be civilized enough, I asked: "Am I the only gentleman Frances has ever brought home?" Ann hesitated, and then, I believe, flat-out lied to protect her sister. "Oh, no," she said. "You're probably the third or fourth. Yes, probably the third or fourth. But you're certainly the most fun." I gave her a look that was intended to quash undue flattery. "You are!" she said. The coquette I'd heard about emerged. "What, you can't take a compliment? A big man like you?" (I know that our taste in women often diverges, but neither of us would get in a fight over Ann. The fire she has is sheer petulance and wounded vanity, I think, not true passion.)

I dared not tell Frances that I couldn't keep her aunts' names straight either. "So Frances tells us that you teach," said Aunt Helen. Or Mary, or Peggy. All nervous with purpose — paying you the utmost attention but behind their eyes troubled by a sheet somewhere that needs hospital corners. Three notes chiming together in a chord. "How do you like it?" they asked. "And you're from Boston? Why, where's your accent? What do your parents do? How do you like our Philadelphia? Frances tells us you're an only child. Have we split your eardrums yet? We bought a bottle of aspirin just for you, it's in the medicine cabinet. Frances tells us you like roast beef, so we had Mary make her special one. Frances must not be cooking for you, otherwise you'd be green around the gills." (Had she even told them about my hospitalization? She must not have, I concluded. When I asked her about it later, she neither confirmed nor denied and instead said, "That's none of their business.") Then, a joke after dinner. One of the aunts brought out a towering flaked coconut cake, set it down without ceremony, said, "Now, who wants some dessert?" and began serving. Then another aunt brought out a rectangular slab of what looked like spiced meat, gray in the main but crisped brown at the edges, set it down next to the cake, and started to carve it up. "Bernard," this other aunt said, putting a slice of this on my plate, "you're having scrapple for dessert. Frances said you'd love it." Laughter all round. "Oh, give him the cake," someone said. I refused it. Then a husband of one of her cousins, who I believe might have been a fireman, ate some along with me in sympathy. I made a big show of enjoying it. Damned if I had two slices. It's actually quite good. As I put the last forkful of it in my mouth, Frances gave me the most caressing look she's ever given me.

Her father drove us to the train station after dinner. While Frances was off buying a paper, he turned to me. I saw sympathy, intelligence, and curiosity in his face, as well as, I am fairly sure, approval. He's a head shorter than me but he's broad-shouldered and confident, brusque and pointed in his movements but generous and fluid in his speech, and I can sense the absolute goodness in him. He would have been a priest, I think, had he perhaps had the intractability of his daughter. Whatever makes Frances indefatigable, she must get it from him. Whatever makes her intractable must come from her mother and the aunts. "That cake is off-limits!" I'd heard one bellow from the kitchen. "I'm assuming you're attracted to the idea of an early death?" I have no doubt she was talking to a man.

"I think it's nice, you two," her father said at the train station. "I think it's nice, two writers. I bet you keep each other good company." "We do," I said.

Frances returned. "Bring her home again soon," he said. "We miss her dearly."

I watched her embrace her father — she shut her eyes, the better to commit this moment to memory, I suppose, should it turn out to be their last, and hung on to him for a few long seconds in a way that made me think she'd throw herself in front of a train for him. I was, of course, jealous. I was also jealous because she had a father who was not afraid of what he did not understand and who would find a way to talk to you about it. I don't think you'll be surprised when I tell you how difficult it was to be around people who made a point to weave themselves together because they had poured out their blood among one another. They may be annoyed with each other, but they do not hate each other. They understand that annoyance is a fair price to pay for the strange protective love of family. I do not often covet what other people have, but I did find myself wishing that I had known something like it.

I saw also that Frances is perfectly suited to family life, that she swims about her people like a fish in their waters, that she is happy when she bathes in their love and their noise, and I think she knows this about herself, that she could quite easily spend her days cooking, cleaning, and corralling children, that she could quite easily be charmed into a life in which she gave order to other lives, not words, and I think this is why she is so strict with herself on the point of marriage. She does not know anyone who has written and mothered, so she thinks it impossible. (I actually don't either — all the women writers I know are libertines.) But she needs to be in control, and she has chosen to be in control of the people in her stories.

We stood on the platform. "Thank you very, very much," she said. I got another caressing look. No sign of intractable Frances. Was it the exhaustion of having successfully fought her way through one of the most difficult maneuvers on the battlefield of romance — the visit home? It's one thing to be able to undo Frances in bed — and I have compromised her there, in telling you that, that's what kind of hold she has on me, that I give a damn about discretion — but it's wholly another for her to, fully clothed and upright, make her preference for me known. Then another caressing look. I am sure she was trying to tell me that she loved me. I didn't know what to say, which alarmed me. I was exhilarated, but could not speak.

She said hardly anything on the train. But she took my hand, and then fell asleep, her head resting on my shoulder. I wanted to propose to her.

I love her. But no sign from her that she's as in love with me. If she were another sort of woman I might suspect her of having someone else in the wings. And I'm not even competing with God for her hand! That I might find acceptable.

Apologies for the length. But that's what you get for not living near me at this crucial juncture. And I had to keep writing because there's a girl from Texas here who's been giving me the eye over the past hour as I sit in the dining hall, and as long as I'm writing she won't come and talk to me. I'm trying to be worthy of my impossible love.

Love,
Bernard

August 15, 1960

Dear Claire —

This will be a very short letter because I have to polish a story before Monday. But I wanted to tell you that Bernard paid a visit to Philadelphia last week, and he was a very big hit. The rotter.

My father, after dinner, took me out back to tell me that if he died, he would not mind leaving me in Bernard's hands. It was a little unnerving. I wanted to ask him if perhaps this was an excess of feeling due to the fact that I'd never brought anyone home before, but I think he really meant it. My aunts exclaimed over him as if he were Errol Flynn. "Jeez, Frances," said Ann. "You sure do know how to make up for lost time." (I have to admit some glee in making Ann a little jealous.) A small cousin of mine demanded to run her toddler hands through his hair, and he let her, grinning like an idiot all the while. That girl was delighted to be in his arms, and she made a big, unselfconscious fuss of showing it.

I was a little chastised. No man should give of himself the way he does to me and receive mere acquiescence in return. It was a lesson, seeing him bear up so good-naturedly under all that noise and fuss and behave as a perfect gentleman in the middle of the circus I come from. What kind of Christian am I if I can't make my appreciation known? What kind of woman?

I find I do miss him now that he's away. I'm a little bored with all the little things I do to plump my nest — do the laundry, clean the kitchen, organize my drafts, flip through cookbooks, draw up a budget, go for walks. It's all starting to seem like an old maid's cross-stitching.

My love to Bill as he girds up for another tour of duty with Seneca et al.

Love,
Frances

August 21, 1960

Bernard —

With you away it's like the Empire State Building's gone out. Come home sooner than soon.

xx Frances

August 27, 1960

My love —

I have your postcard resting on the windowsill in front of my desk. I read it several times a day. I slip it in whatever book I am reading by the pond to use as a bookmark and read it a few more times in the sun. Even though I have removed myself from you I am still distracted. But I wrote twenty solid lines today and know that there will be probably a hundred more before I leave, so here I am, drinking whiskey and luxuriating in the thought of you.

What I miss most of all is your face, flushed and happy, after you come. Eyes bright like a girl with a secret she can't bear to keep.

I want you flushed and happy, and then I want you on my lap afterward, naked, warmed by the sun coming through the window, both of us coming back into our speaking selves, my kiss on your shoulders as you talk of some story you saw transpire on the subway that morning.

I want you on the street in a dress an hour later, quiet, sated, taking my hand as we walk to dinner. You in your white lace dress, your hair a little damp around your cheeks, still sweaty from the bedroom and sweaty from the heat, something succulent but starched. I will wear my wrinkled khakis and a short-sleeved work shirt that I have refused to let you iron, and I will lead us through the carnival that is the Village, knowing that we may appear as chaste as the maiden and her unicorn but smiling in triumph because you are my secret I can't bear to keep, my beatific girl, all mine to kiss wherever and however I please.

What a perfect summer we had.

When I come back to New York, I will not let you out of my sight.

All my love,
Bernard

September 23, 1960

Ted —

Throw this away if you can't be bothered. I wanted these thoughts and deeds on paper so I could see exactly what kind of ass I have been. Then I wanted to exorcise the whole thing by destroying the evidence, but burning it seemed histrionic, and throwing it out not extermination enough — so I decided to mail it to you. You will have something to say about this, and I know what it will be, so don't trouble yourself with a reply.

I said a cruel thing to Frances. We were, of course, at a party — a party thrown by Margaret, Russell's wife. Frances does not like Margaret much — I think she thinks Margaret is an empty chinoiserie vase of a woman, too brittle and gilded for her tastes — and I think she was made diffident by having to be there.

Now, I must first blame Margaret before blaming Frances. No: I must first blame someone's wife, I don't know whose, before blaming Margaret. If this wife had not spoken, Frances might not have been moved to say what she did. I left Frances to go find us some drinks, and when I returned this wife was saying: "That's nice, a novel. I had one too, before I got married."

Said Frances: "A novel that vanishes probably should not have existed in the first place."

I knew then that the evening was officially over. I excused us by saying we had to go say hello to the hostess. Frances, insulted by the wife's insinuation that she was on the road to noble failure, refused to say a word to anyone who stopped to talk to us. Which angered me more and more as the night went on. I felt it was a refusal to think of how she might reflect on me, and therefore a refusal to think of herself as belonging to me. Comes along Margaret, who ignores Frances to ask if I've seen Jim Schultz lately, which I knew she was asking because she'd been sleeping with him but now he wasn't returning her calls. But Frances cannot stand being snubbed. She thinks there's a verse in Matthew with Christ forbidding it, right after he suffers the little children to come unto him.

I elegantly hedged — I hedged to make it appear as if I had seen him, when really I hadn't, just to torture Margaret. Then Frances finally spoke. "Anyone who sleeps with Jim Schultz is buying a raffle ticket to win the clap."

Margaret stiffened as if shot from behind. "Everybody out!" she shouted. "Out! Out! Thank you for coming!" Thank God the place had been loud enough that no one could detect where the offense had come from. She left us standing where we were and began shoving people in the direction of her bedroom, where the coats were. She pulled two people up from the chairs they were chatting on. A glass shattered. "No, I'm not kidding! Get your things! It is finished! Thank you for coming!"

"Whoops," said Frances as we followed the crowd to the back of the apartment to get our coats. I have to admit that even though I was angry with Frances, the scene was amusing.

Frances waited until we got a few blocks away from the dispersed partiers, until we were standing at the corner of Lexington and Sixty-Third, to speak.

"Why didn't you tell me they were sleeping together?" she said. Her voice was soggy with remorse.

"That was very row home stoop of you," I said. I wanted to punish her for having made an insufficient show of wanting to belong to me.

She grabbed my arm and turned me around to face her, stumbling a little from the effort of trying to force me, losing a shoe in the process. The city, hanging blackly cavernous about her, and this man who loves her turning on her. She bent down, picked up the shoe, and threw it at me. Then she hailed a cab. "We don't even have a stoop, you bastard," she said, and got in. I fell in love with her again.

The next day, at the end of the day, I showed up at her office with the shoe in a paper bag and a red scratch down my right temple where the heel had scraped me. I stood in her doorway, manifesting the air of a penitent thief. She was not manifesting the air of clemency. Without saying a word, she got up from her desk and walked out the door, her skirts brushing against my knees. After five minutes she came back, grabbed her purse and coat, shut the lights off with me standing there, and left. I followed her out to the elevators.

She would not look at me once we were down on the street. "I know you didn't mean what you said," she said as we walked. "You couldn't possibly." And then: "If you are excited by me throwing a shoe at you, please know that it does not excite me."

She was lying about that.

The subject was dropped.

I am finding it hard not to insult her in other ways.

Dear Claire —

Bernard and I have had what I suppose you would call a fight. Well, we have had two fights. I will not tell you about the one that ended in me throwing my shoe at him.

We were at a party, two nights ago. It was crowded, and dark, and loud, and when he got tired of shouting over the crowd, Bernard started to kiss me. I stopped him. I didn't want him to kiss me in public. Bernard argued that no one would care what we did; I argued that he should care about what I thought. We argued some more — I think he may have told me to grow up. I have been feeling that he is trying to make a request of me in these two fights but he will not name it. I walked away from him in the middle of something he was saying. I put my coat on and walked out on the street and got a cab. The second time in a month. I heard him call my name. That is one of the things I love about New York. If you wish to get away from an unpleasant situation immediately, there are cabs everywhere, ready to make you feel, at least for five minutes, that you are having the last word, by way of the very satisfying sound of a slammed car door.

Bernard followed me home. He must have taken a cab too, because he got there shortly after I arrived. I was sitting on the couch reading and waiting for the kettle blow for tea when I heard a whistle from down on the street. About thirty seconds passed. Then I heard what I thought was a coin thrown at the window. And then another. And another. I opened the window. Bernard was standing there, hands in his pockets. He was wearing the face of a child looking up at a clock that he fears might tell him that he has missed his train. "Will you let me up?" he said. I saw the child he must have been, the child of a woman who let her mother-in-law name her baby because he was a boy, not a girl, and she was too disappointed by that fact to care what he was called. I did as he asked.

I closed the door behind us. I didn't say anything. We looked at each other. "Why don't you love me?" he said.

"That's not it," I said. Silence. "Bernard, you know I did not grow up being petted," I said.

"Neither did I, Frances," he said. "Do you think God wants you to love this way?"

"No," I said.

"No one will love you like I love you," he said. What do you do when you know this is true? I'm a thirteen-year-old girl with vinegar where my blood should be. He came toward me and I found my back against the front door. He moved in closer and took hold of my arms. I thought he might shake me but he stood very still. He tightened his grip. "Marry me," he said. I couldn't believe that he didn't see that proposing to a woman when her back was literally against a wall was not a harbinger of a happy union. "No!" I said. I sounded shrill, like a patient panicked by the approach of a needle. I'm not proud of that. As if I thought raising my voice would wake him up and stop him from making this mistake. He pushed me up against the door. "Let me go," I said. He did. "I think you should go," I said, and he did.

I've called him at work and at home, but I haven't heard from him. I went to his apartment last night and rang the buzzer and no answer. I can't sleep.

Frances

October 27, 1960

Dear Claire —

I am writing this to you from Payne Whitney, where Bernard is now staying, while I wait for visiting hours to begin. I thought about calling you but I don't trust myself to speak coherently about this.

I stayed late at work to write two Thursdays ago and when I came home — this was about eight o'clock — I found Bernard lying on his back on the street, asleep, mouth open, outside the door to my building. I had not seen him since we'd fought. (The college hadn't seen him either, I have since learned.) I walked upstairs, called the police, and asked if they would take him home. I told them they would need a few extra men because he would probably put up a fight. Then I went back down the stairs and sat on the street beside him. He smelled like a dog who'd been drinking from a mud puddle made of whiskey and ashes. I looked at his hair. I wanted to finger some tangles loose but I thought that if stirred, he'd become violent. So I sat there listening to him breathe, praying he'd stay asleep until the police arrived. Mostly we were ignored, but one woman walking by, loaded down with shopping bags and wearing the kind of shoes my grandmother used to wear, frowned right at me and muttered, "Damn beatniks." When the police came, I stood up and backed away and they got to work. "Where is she?" Bernard said. "Where is she?" "She doesn't want to talk to you, sir," one officer said, and I wish he hadn't. He was very young, short, with jug ears and black hair slicked back with a heavy hand. I bet he had sisters who used to beat him up. They started to try to pack Bernard into the car, and, as expected, he sent someone to the ground with a punch, and then the officers clotted around him like blood in a wound, cuffing his hands behind him and wrestling him to the pavement, chest down, an officer's foot on his back. I thought of Saint George with his foot on the dragon. I noticed people gathering behind the police to watch. Then Bernard saw me. He gave me a look of pure hatred. "I am the vine," he said, "and you are my bride. You think I am the serpent but I am the vine, and because you are lukewarm I will spit you out of my mouth."

And then he said: "The dragon has his foot on the saint, but soon I will send my son and he will wrestle the dragon and the bride will rise up to meet me."

I couldn't help but think he had read my mind. A chill went through me so quickly and deeply it left me nauseated. "We need to take him to Bellevue, I think," I told the police. "He's my friend; I'm not his family. What do I need to do?" They said they would take him and then call another car for me. I told them no, that I would ride with Bernard, but they wouldn't let me. "Miss," said a cop, bleary but firm, "you can tell him you love him when he's done thinking he's Jesus." Everybody was reading my mind. I went back upstairs and called John Percy, who said he'd meet me at the hospital. Another cop came back and then drove me over. I cried in the car. I prayed that God would guard me against the egotism that is guilt. The cop kept driving and said nothing. He bought me a cup of coffee at a grocery before taking me inside.

Bernard has now been at Payne Whitney two weeks. (It is more than a little sepulchral in here.) Sullivan told me to take November off, that he could get a niece of his to fill in. So I have been visiting Bernard every day. We don't talk much. I read to him, or we take whatever walk we can. I ended up teaching him how to play hearts. Sometimes we will just sit next to each other, and he will put his hand on my knee and then attempt to kiss my forehead, with varying degrees of accuracy. I am trying for once in my life to shut up and see what that is like. I think Bernard might be trying an experiment like that himself.

The day before yesterday he put his head in my lap. After a while he began to cry. A nurse, overhearing him on her way down the hall, came in and whispered to me that I should probably go for the day. When she pulled him away from me, he slid onto the floor and stayed there, crying. She nodded to me — if a nod could be said to be wise and absolving, this one was — and then turned her back and knelt down to him. In that moment I felt as if someone had rolled a stone over a tomb, and I would always be standing outside that tomb, deaf to the pain within. I called Peter from a pay phone in a hallway and I got drunk in the Village — the first time in my life I got drunk on purpose. I did not even think about going to a church. Apparently at the end of the evening I kept telling Peter I was no good, no god-damn earthly good. Final proof, in case I was wondering, that I am indeed and irrevocably Irish.

How many hospitals will I be writing you from?

I wish you were here.

Love,
Frances

November 23, 1960

Dear Frances —

This is for you to read on the train home to your family.

There are several ways I want to begin this letter, and I can't decide which one to take up.

So I will begin with the abject: Forgive me.

My love for you is real. It is much more real than the love I had for God. When I think of you going about your life innocently and in full freedom and then being conscripted into my madness, I want to commit myself to an institution forever. How can I ever atone for having distorted you into an allegory?

My madness is also real, but it is not as real as my love for you.

There is no one in this world who delights me as you do. Your mind is sturdily aflame, your thoughts constantly at a temperature that will scald the sleepers. You think with your mind and your soul, which is why those thoughts burn the way they do. I love you because of it. And I want the responsibility of making you incarnate. You say you do not want to marry but I think that is an attempt to escape the tedious daily struggle to love another human being. (I think this explains some of your antipathy toward teaching too.) If you remain alone in the city, your only duties will be to your writing and to God, and those duties take the form we want them to take. We give them the shape we understand, even when we think we are giving them dominion over us. To wit: you go to Mass daily but sit right in front, so as not to have to witness the mass delusion that is the rote childish piety of little old ladies.

Frances, you feel like a home to me. When you whisper my name, the world becomes still, and I with it.

I know I've gone about saying these things in the wrong way — this is what I meant when I asked you to marry me. It came out as a command because I was frightened of losing you.

I would not ask you to have a family — I realize that with my illness I am child enough for you. We will have your family fill our house with their lively warmth; we will have our friends do the same.

I ask for you to have faith that God wants you for me in addition to himself. Please have faith that God is putting me in your way because he thinks you are capable of loving more than you have ever known.

Please be as brave as I think you are.

Bernard

December 1, 1960

Dear Bernard —

I have been thinking of all you have written, and all we have said.

I am moving back to Philadelphia. I am doing this to put distance between us, and also because I learned over the holiday that Ann is pregnant.

I will never be able to be the wife you need, and it would be too painful for me to remain your friend while you fall in love with the woman who really should be your wife. So I am going to ask that we stop speaking to each other.

I do believe you when you say that you feel your love for me is more real than your madness, but I am afraid that for me, standing outside your illness, your madness might eclipse your love. I think, too, that your disease is a gift, even as it is an awful burden, because when you are not ill, you move forward with a fever that is a shadow of your mania, and that fever gives you poems, and teaching, and storytelling, and the ability to argue your love for me. I do not have an equivalent engine. It would require all of my spirit to take care of you the way you need to be taken care of — the way I wish I could take care of you, which would be the way God would require me to take care of you if I were to become your wife. There would be no spirit left for my books.

I have left work in the middle of several days to sit in St. Patrick's and pray about this, and whenever I get up from the paddock I feel an undeniable rock in my gut weighing me down and away from marriage. It is, I think, a heaviness from God. Writing is the only thing I feel at peace while doing. If I were taken from it, I would be a bitter, bitter woman.

I am going to trust that you want my books to be in the world as much as you want me to be in the world, and I pray you can keep their well-being in mind.

I hope I can forget how much I love you.

Frances

$\backsim$

May 15, 1961

Dear Claire —

Thank you for coming to visit. Ann in particular liked having you here. And my father, even through his senility, could tell you were something special. "Have her back," he said. "You should have her back. It's nice for you girls to have someone to play with."

I wish you could come more often. I am now beginning to see why people marry. It's necessary to have a bulwark against family — to have someone who is not imprisoned in the insanity and yet is close enough to it that his or her observations on the inmate population have the ring of objectivity. Although I would not want to put a husband through this. I was short-tempered enough with my father before I was forced to admit that the senility I suspected was the truth, and I fear that I would foist the short-temperedness onto a husband. Peggy, however, says that I am still young and that I shouldn't say things like that. I used to turn incredibly sour when my aunts told me what I shouldn't say, but now I find their voices comforting. These people are stronger than me. They cry at the drop of a hat, but they're still stronger than me. I think their proficiency in emotion means that they will never be undone by it.

Thank you also for coming to talk to my classes about newspaper reporting. These girls never let their enthusiasm show, but they were, pretty much all of them, sitting at attention as you talked. Of course:

you were a living Weegee photo, and usually I am trying to get them to see that an opinion is not an argument. They're perfectly pleasant, as you saw, but these girls, many of whom should just ditch the pretense of college and marry themselves off immediately, show a distressing incomprehension of their mother tongue on paper. It's the way I am with French — I can speak it and read it, but please don't make me write it. I stand around with bunches of *ys* and *dus* in my hand, scratching my head and wondering where to plug up the holes. They have as much trouble with the possessive apostrophe as I have with the rascally prepositions and articles of French. But I have to say, teaching is, and I can't quite believe this, something I enjoy. It is a losing battle, but unlike the losing battle of tending to my father and his illness, I can see just enough enlightenment in their eyes to make me want to show up to the next class. Of course, I also like being in charge and being paid for it.

That letter from Bernard that came just as you were leaving contained news of his engagement. He felt he should tell me so that I did not hear it from John or other mouths. This girl is someone who interviewed him a while ago for a magazine. She works at the Morgan, I guess, as some sort of curator or librarian, and she lives in the city too. He said very little about her other than that. I met her twice before I left the city, and if I remember her right, she's tall, black-haired, white-skinned, somewhat beautiful. I think she's black Irish, from lawyers, and those Irish have always fascinated — as mine have been fitfully to modestly employed, bards given laryngitis by the superstructure. The second time I met her was at a party, and she had an expensive-looking dress on, gray tweed, shaped modestly but dramatically with simple, severe lines, and she was listening intently to another guest. A friend of mine. When the friend saw me, he called me over. He introduced me to her and she smiled, very quickly and tightly, and I got the sense that smiling for her was as devoid of meaning as sneezing. I wondered if she remembered the first time we met. I think she did.

She did seem no-nonsense, which is good for him. I remember looking at her in that dress and thinking that there was something of a dog trainer about her, and that if you stepped out of line, she would very easily get you to heel. It must have been the tweed dress and the patient listening and the hair in a bun. Young Elizabeth at Balmoral, etc. I could say this only to you, but while I am shocked at how soon this all happened, I am relieved that he is happily paired off.

I read back over this and I hear self-pity. Claire, forgive me. I ask God every day to help me look at my father the way he looks at me now — with some joy merely because here is someone with whom to have coffee and look at the birds. Sitting with him and watching the birds is not spending time with my father. It's paying respects to a monument. No teasing, no stories from him. No laughter when I tell him how I put some functionary or other in his place, because I don't tell him those things anymore. I just have to sit there, telling myself that I am loving him by paying him respect for having raised me. There's no real pleasure in it. There's a great deal of anger and sadness, because my father with all his particulars has now faded into a philosophical problem: How should we love those whom we have loved for their particulars when those particulars are no longer present? I don't mind God being a philosophical problem — I never thought of him as my heavenly father anyway — but I don't want Frank Reardon to be.

I used to think *Story of a Soul* was not really Thérèse's autobiography but a novel for children — its heroine so ludicrously good, like Pollyanna, that you had to wonder if someone had made her up as a parody of the genre and sniggered as she did it. (I admit, I sniggered when I read it.) But I no longer laugh at Thérèse and her Little Way. It helps with the students. And I am using her to endure the *Ed Sullivan Show*. The trick here is to be hemming something or grading papers while it airs. The other night when the theme song klaxoned up like an air-raid siren, and I settled into the couch alongside my father, Ann made a crack as she ate her third bowl of ice cream that evening. "I think the real show," she said to me, finishing off a spoonful, "is you being able to sit through this without drinking."

All my love again,
Frances

May 16, 1961

Ted—

I have so many times forced you to do favors for me—I am writing now to formally ask one of you.

You are not as excited as I'd hoped you would be about my marriage. I know that we will remain friends above it, because you have been a witness to all my mistakes, but I am asking you to try to be kind to her. I know she can be cold initially, but I think the more you know her, the more you will appreciate her. She loves Trollope almost as much as you do. Could you start there? About her coldness—I think she may be sensing that you are measuring her against someone else, and when she senses that, or senses that she is in a roomful of people who are acutely aware that she is not someone else, she shuts people out in defense, before they have a chance to shut her out. With three sentences she can split my mind like the atom, and the words I need tumble forth, and forth, with the speed and heat I need from them. Her intelligence never fails. It organizes and protects; it clears paths for heart's ease. I think this unrepentant steadiness has tamed me. You yourself have remarked upon the change. So I am asking that you trust that we will love each other as long as we can and that you'll be generous of spirit, which is your nature, when you are around her.

Bernard

May 16, 1961

Dear John —

I hope you are enjoying Miami. Very perverse and un-Percy, a vacation in Miami. I send my regards to Julia and her family. Peel an orange on a patio for me.

I am writing to tell you that I have proposed to Susan. I suppose I could have told you when you returned to the city, but I am very happy and did not want to wait. My mother approves. "Has he told you that he's been in mental institutions?" she asked Susan at dinner one night. Susan said yes, and my mother said, "Well, it's up to you now to make sure he doesn't get back in there, you know." "Bernard's a man," said Susan, "not a dog, Mrs. Eliot," and do you know, my mother laughed? "Susan," she later told me, "will not put up with your nonsense." I am thinking she made this leap purely because Susan showed she would not put up with my mother's own damn nonsense, but it's true, Susan does not put up with my nonsense, and I am enjoying this reprieve from my mother's almighty glower. Susan says my mother wants an adversary but doesn't want her power dimmed by mine or sapped by my father's, which is why she can show Susan affection even as she is challenged by her. This is what I have thought since childhood. Also, Susan knows how to play up to my mother's vanity, in the subtlest of ways, so I don't have to.

My father says that Susan is a pretty girl with a good head on her shoulders. For what that's worth.

We're going to get married at city hall next month. I have written to Frances to tell her. I know you said that it would not be a good idea to write to her, but I thought she should hear it from me before she heard it from anyone else. I don't expect to hear back. I did not, of course, mention that you had told me about her father's senility. If any one thing would move me to take up prayer again, it is the thought of Frances losing her father's recognition.

Please write when you can.

Yours,
Bernard

May 23, 1961

Dear John —

How is New York? You know, I did not think I would miss it when I left to come back to Philadelphia, but I do. I miss the endless variety of faces to be studied on the subway, for one. Please also say hello to Julia.

You were so kind to write and see if I was writing. I am not, currently. Five stories finished but nothing else seems to be coming to mind. I would like to write two or three more by the end of the year, but I think I might squeeze just one more out of these next six months. What is strange is that I am not bothered by the fact that my brain feels like a Dust Bowl farmhouse left vacant after the Depression. But do you know there's a pleasantness to it? I am imagining my mind as the upper room before the disciples piled in, readying itself for the Holy Ghost. I am trusting that something will come rushing in at some point soon. I'm reading a lot, though, because I've been teaching, have just finished teaching, English-survey courses at my alma mater, Germantown College — or, as I like to call it, the College of Mary Pat. Being that there are so many of them — Mary Pats, that is. It's a very small girls' school run by the Sisters of Saint

Joseph in a town just north of the city. They asked me to come teach for them, and I could not afford to turn them down. Reading and talking about reading for money made more sense than writing ridiculous ad copy for money. I never expected to feel warmth toward a bunch of nuns — my reflex when confronted with a bunch of nuns, as you know, is to wish for a trapdoor to open up right under my feet — but warmth is what I find myself feeling at the College of Mary Pat. These nuns have read enough to cure themselves of superstition and spite. They hired me knowing exactly what my novel was about, so they really must be cured of it. Although one sister did say to me, at a tea for parents, that she had read my book, and then told me: "I was angry like you when I was young, but after a while the Holy Spirit took that anger away from me." I changed the subject. There is another sister, in her sixties, who teaches French and who swims every morning in the pool of a neighboring military academy. I think we have become friends. She asked me to introduce her to Kierkegaard, and we are reading *Diary of a Seducer* together. She has introduced me to Balzac. Where has he been all my life? I know: buried under Tolstoy.

Thank you also for asking after my father and sister. My father — senility is terrible, but it is especially terrible in that his doctor says there is nothing physically wrong with him. And that is what it seems like. So my father is fine. My sister is fine as well. She's been working nights at Whitman's chocolate factory. She takes care of my father during the day, and I take care of him at night when she goes off to her shift. And then my aunts help us along. If you do ever want to leave New York for a day, we would love to have you. I would like to introduce you to Sister Josephine, she of the morning swims.

Thank you again for writing to me. Your letter was cheering.

Yours,
Frances

Dear Claire —

Thank you for your letter, and for the recipes from the test kitchens of the *Tribune*. Ann would like me to tell you that she thanks you too, because she's getting tired of my weeknight reliance on hamburger. She's getting tired of a lot of things, but that is her right as a pregnant lady.

What would I do without you? When I get a letter from you I rejoice, because it means there is wisdom in this world, and it did not get wiped out by the automobile.

I wanted to write and tell you that Ann will be marrying Michael. He's always been respectful to everyone here, and she tells me he's devoted to his mother. (*Al Capone was devoted to his mother too*, I wanted to say.) She's dated a series of salesmen — Ann and her appetite for flash — so her dating a man with an actual trade might mean that she knew what she was doing with this one.

But the fact that he did not propose right away when she found out she was pregnant worries me. The night he came over to do it, I took him into the kitchen between coffee and dessert, sat him down at the table, and told him that he did not need to marry her if he didn't love her, because her aunts and I would take care of her. He looked straight at me and said that they loved each other. What can you say to that? If a person looks straight at you with solemn eyes and says he loves your sister, and you see your sister suffering because she has not been proposed to, and you think the suffering may be because she is afraid she might lose someone she loves, not because she would be without material support — then you have to let him back out into the dining room to finish his coffee.

We are going to his parents' house for dinner next week. His mother — her name is Theresa — telephoned and invited us all over. Her tone was determined and cheerful without being unctuously chipper. This invitation is a good sign, I think — it means that they are not going to punish them, or us, for this. Ann seems happier now. In a way, it's good my father is senile and has no idea what is happening, because I think he would be more wounded than Ann is by how her marriage came about.

Since Ann is out of some danger for now, I will worry about her only when I absolutely have to. And I can actually read again. My love, by the way, to Bill. Tell him I just bought *The Magic Mountain* and I am going to start in on it.

Love,
Frances

October 15, 1962

Dear Ted—

I hope being in Los Angeles for a month overseeing depositions is not destroying you. I think I myself could take Los Angeles for only a month before I converted back to Catholicism again in revolt against its surfaces. But I'd love that first month. The sun like a punishment from a god. This is a thinly veiled request for you to invite me out there.

A few weeks ago I went to a party for Harrow. I told you this when you called the other day. What I didn't tell you was that I saw Frances while I was there. Why did I not tell you this? I remembered the forbidding stare you gave me last Christmas when I began a sentence with her name. I am telling you now because I am in some tumult.

She was in town visiting John and giving a reading for the new book, and we ran into each other. I had no idea she would be there. Although if I'd thought twice about it, I would have admitted it was a possibility. She was there with John's wife, Julia, and a woman John had just signed up. I wanted to congratulate her — because that book most definitely deserves congratulations, and it deserves one of these corrupt awards and if they put me on the committee next year I am going to demand that they nominate it — but she was avoiding me, I could tell. I walked in and we caught each other's eye — she was standing right near the bar with Julia and this woman — and after I checked my coat, I went back to find her, but she was gone. Every time I was freed from a conversation, I walked around the party trying to find her, and every time I found her, there she was, entangled in some conversation herself, and I'd send her a look inviting her to step outside that conversation, but then she would slip away from that knot, and I would have to go find her again. It took four attempts, but I finally cornered her. She was nervous. She kept drinking her drink, even after she'd drunk it down to the ice. I told her I wanted to say hello to her and congratulate her and she tilted the drink back one tilt too far so that the ice fell out of her glass and ran down her dress. "Oh, for God's sake," she said. And then she laughed. "How are you?" she said, casually, as if it had been a week since she'd seen me, not almost two years. "How does it feel to be nominated for such an illustrious award?" she said. She was not ready to be genuinely interested in me.

So I decided to force us into honesty. "I do miss you," I said. And that was true. I didn't think it would cost us anything for me to say it.

She waited a moment or two, and then said: "It was as if you were dead." *It was as if* — voice rising up onto its toes on the *if,* putting the accent on that syllable, and then a pause before coming back down to deliver the blow —*you were dead.* She took a drink again but there was still nothing in the glass. Frances cannot pull off hauteur. Her secret vice of self-hatred makes itself known.

Then one of the publicists came by, a girl who John lets do his dirtiest work, clearly intoxicated from drink. "Bernard Eliot! Bernard Eliot!" she said. I stared at her with a thunderous glare, hoping that she would move along. She turned to Frances. "Isn't she a love?" she said to me. "Such a love!" Frances looked as if she wanted to strangle this girl. "Yes," I said, conscripting myself into chivalry. "Who doesn't love Frances?" I meant it, but it did come out a little curdled around the edges. And the publicist took off, leaving the two of us staring at each other.

There is something about Frances still that makes me want to court her. And she's the one who left me! Just seeing her — she looked just the same, as bright as a bunch of day lilies sprung up erect and chaste in the middle of an unkempt lawn, growing erect and green, green and apart from everything dull — made me want to pay her the tribute of my undivided attention. What did I do, after she tried unsuccessfully to make me think she was doing just fine? I took up chivalry again and offered to take her out for a drink. "May I take you out for a drink?" I said. "Yes," she replied, after thinking about it. And her eyes did appear to soften. "Let's go to the St. Regis," I said. I got our coats and led her out by the hand. She took her hand away, and then I grabbed it again. Ted, I know what you are thinking. But remember you have had your own temptations.

At the St. Regis, it took a while for her to relax. She sat on her stool like a parakeet perched on the bar in its cage. She sat holding her beauty to herself in the complacent, oblivious way old women hug their purses to their laps on the subway. All those New York women around her, thoroughbreds whinnying at the gate, and: Frances. Everything that was so beloved to me about the whiteness of her skin, pure and undulating, freckled and plush, came back in an instant as she lifted her chin to drink. I had to talk to shake it off. I told her about you, told her about teaching, told her what I was thinking of writing next, told her what I thought of her book, went on and on about her book. I felt that she was looking at me for hints of decrepitude. Looking and sipping her drink, and I realized again what I have thought many times since then, which is that she was sent by God to show me myself. "Bernard," she finally said, finally giving up the chill, putting a hand on my arm, "you do not need to keep talking." I brought her hand to my lips and that was the end of it. I told her to put her coat on. "Oh, no no no no no," she said. But I dragged her by the hand again, out to the street, hailed a cab, and told the cabdriver to drive us to Coney Island and back, that I'd pay him three times the tab for his trouble, and on the return trip into the city I tried to force myself on her, but of course she stopped me. She had never let me get away with that in a cab before, and she wouldn't let me now.

In the cab outside her hotel she started crying. She was trying to hide it but I saw tears on her face. "What's wrong?" I said. "I didn't know how much I would miss you," she said. "Well, write me," I said. "There's no harm in writing." "I don't know," she said. Then the cabdriver said: "Mister, I don't want to have to charge you four times the fare for this trip." She laughed. "Goodbye," she said, and then she ran up the stairs of her hotel and into her lobby without looking back. I wondered if I had made her do something she didn't want to do. But there was some note of query in her response to me — something leaf-green and nascent at the bottom of her deep blue reserve.

We drove to my building, and I felt an inexpressible sadness when I got out of the cab. I stood there on York Avenue in front of the apartment, reluctant to go in. I almost hailed another cab back to Frances's hotel. I started cursing her for getting in the cab with me. I did not want to sleep next to Susan. I slept on the couch and masturbated, cursing both Susan and Frances. The next morning Susan said: "Is something wrong?" I said no, nothing. She did not believe me, but since I was coming home every night, made sure to come home every night, she let the subject drop.

I do miss her. I even miss her rigidity. It is a self-containment that to me mimics the sublime. It's not hysterical, as Susan's now seems — and that's unfair, because I've made Susan hysterical. Looking at Frances, I had the realization that I had been both her lover and her brother. With most people, you settle into being one or the other. I feel related to her still, familial, because she knew me when

I was at my most Bernard and I knew her when she was at her most Frances. We'd read each other like books we were endlessly fascinated by. Frances, of course, hiding her fascination beneath the covers of intellectual exchange and perhaps some subconscious notion that we were enacting a holy friendship like that of Teresa of Ávila and John of the Cross.

She is — was — the familial and yet the sublime.

I am determined for once in my life not to hurt a woman if I can help it. I know I will do it again in a rage, but while I am sane at this moment, I want to be good — that insipid word which should be sacred. And yet I feel myself wanting to see what Frances is like now, see if this pliancy I sense in her is softness or sadness, and I tell myself that if I undertook this mission, it would be sacred because it's Frances — it would be forgiven by the laws of God and man because it is Frances. If I wrote her, I know that I would be trying to get her in front of me again so I could consume as much of her as she would allow. A panic is gathering, a clutch of wild conjecture that's sending me out walking for hours between teaching and home, and I don't know whether it means I have to reach toward her or turn away from her, or check myself in somewhere. No, I know I don't need to be checked in somewhere — I have a very clear sense here that I am a moral animal. I half wish that I were about to break down so I would not need to feel that burden.

Bernard

October 16, 1962

Dear Bernard —

I hope this letter finds you well. I was glad to see you. You might not have been able to tell, but I was. Very much so.

You suggested I write. I am about to start two classes on Milton.

Maybe you could tell me what I shouldn't miss in pitching my soft-balls to the girls at the College of Mary Pat.

Thank you for reading my book.

Yours,
Frances

November 12, 1962

Frances —

Dear Frances.

I don't think we should write each other. Starting up a correspon-dence with you would be too dangerous for me.

Susan saw your return address on the envelope, which she found in a book that I'd left in the kitchen — I should have been more care-ful about this, it's true, because she is a ruthless tidier — and she went out of her mind in a way that was difficult to witness.

I want to explain to you why I am saying this. Susan is extremely jealous of you. She has not been jealous of the women I have taken up with when I have been ill. She understood that those girls really were just wreckage from episodes — minor players in a nightmare — but if she thought I were about to start a dalliance with you, she would think something else entirely. She would think I had changed my mind in broad daylight, while sane, and that my love for her had truly disappeared. I remember you once wrote me that you could judge like an Irish mother-in-law. Well, Susan, I think, may have you beat there. She is hysterically jealous for this reason: When she and I had been together for five months, we were at a reading. I was off some-where, I forget where, and Susan got stuck talking to the assistant that John had to fire because he caught her writing a novel at her desk (I can hear you now — *Doesn't that girl know she needs to get hired by an octogenarian if she wants to keep up that sort of thing?*). This girl told Susan that she used to work for John and, not knowing who Susan was, and I think in an attempt to proffer some impressive cocktail party gossip, said that she'd once overheard Julia telling John that she'd always wished you and I would get married. And then the girl went on to say that she always thought the same thing whenever you and I would stop by the office together to say hello; she thought we looked so handsome together, and she thought it was terrible that you'd spurned me — her word — and wasn't it tragic. Susan left the girl without saying a word and dragged me into a corner and told me to come clean about what I felt for you. "If there's some great love you're not over, then we need to end this right now," she said. It did not help that I was laughing a little when she told me the story. You are both the eldest, beloved by your fathers — Jove's gray-eyed daughters, you have known nothing but worship — and you girls do not take kindly to being in second place. My mother is one of them too. I didn't know Susan well enough to feel for her like I should have; instead, I saw her as a character in a story, maybe one of your stories, who, while snared in the comically coincidental, was being served with the uncomfortable truth of comeuppance. "You awful child," she said, and slapped me. It made an impression.

I sent Ted your book and your letters for safekeeping soon after. I do not have them in the house because if I'd kept them, she would think that I'd been lying to her that night. (I had John send your new book to me at Columbia and I am keeping it in my desk here, where she will never look. I am writing you now from Columbia.) I did lie to her that night, because I was ambivalent, but eventually I saw that she loved with constancy. I saw how she tended to her parents and her two brothers. And then things changed. Or, rather, I decided to love her.

I think it's true what you said — that I needed someone to care for me and only me. I didn't see it then but I do see it now. And Susan takes care of me. Her mind latches on to my sentences and can weed out the ones that have turned in on themselves. She keeps the house spotless so that I feel a calm I never felt before — the calm of the order of things and how an order of things radiates a peace — and can hear myself think in a way I haven't before. She has made an art of bullying a hospital staff. It's a bit embarrassing, but I'm thankful.

Do you remember what you wrote to me when we parted? That you wanted me to keep the well-being of your books in mind? Frances, you were right to tell me no. I would have cheated on you the way I have cheated on Susan. What would you have done about that? You said that you have had trouble writing while you've been taking care of your father — what words would you lose if you had to suffer adultery, which would bring indignity along with sorrow? What words would have been swallowed in locking me out of the house in the winter and then dragging me in from the steps in the morning, in calling me at Columbia to make sure I am at Columbia and not somewhere else, in coming to a bar where you have a suspicion I will be with a girl whom you suspect I have slept with, in shouting at me for days and then going silent, your voice hoarse and your heart stopped?

When John sent me your book, I read that first sentence and I thought what I have always thought: *She can do anything.* Do everything, then. Do it without me.

Love,
Bernard

November 20, 1962

Dear Bernard —

So I'm denied the privilege of resuming a dialogue with you because of your wife's juvenile paranoia. I am once more again glad that I have never married.

You are contenting yourself to love someone who appears warm because she works with words, and words are not numbers, but she is, I think, essentially cold, colder than I ever was. I think she loves only herself, according to details that have been passed along to me, unsolicited, as if in condolence — in condolence to me and, by proxy, to you. I knew girls like her in high school. I bet she was one of those girls who pretended to like the nuns and then snickered behind their backs about how they were all probably lesbians, since none of them could summon the courage to tell the nuns straight to their faces that they were full of nonsense. She's like the girls I saw at the nunnery: humorless beautiful girls who made a game of shifting allegiances among the other humorless beautiful girls in order to snatch more men or better jobs. It was blood sport but they were so beautiful and groomed, their hair in chignons, it looked just like ballet. What does she know about the human heart?

Also, Ted tells me she roasts a piece of meat like the Irish girl she is: by boiling it.

Don't worry. I won't ever write you again. If I were as schooled in blood sport as your wife, however, I would have sent this letter to your house.

December 1, 1962

Frances —

Please believe me when I tell you I asked for death several times while writing that letter. I might have written it too quickly and emphasized some feelings at the expense of others, and you might not have known how sincere I was. But you have put me in a difficult position — you are making me feel that I owe you loyalty and certain confessions, but I can't give those things to you. Not only because of what I owe Susan, but because of what I owe you. My intentions might not be worthy of you. I might have seduced you and then asked you to keep your distance, and then where would we be?

I must still feel too many things for you if I ask that we not speak to each other.

Bernard

December 3, 1962

Frances —

I was sitting in my doctor's office waiting for an appointment and I heard the receptionist call out two surnames, one right after the other — Francis, and then Reardon. I looked up and a tall colored gentleman and then a short overweight woman with a cane rose and headed to the back. It was something right out of your books. I felt a sort of premonition, something I have never felt before, when I heard those names, and I needed to know that you were all right.

Bernard

December 8, 1962

Bernard —

Thank you for your concern, but it's really no business of yours any longer how I am doing.

Please do not write me again.

December 15, 1962

Dear Claire —

Would you believe me if I told you I saw Bernard at a party when I went to New York for my reading? Would you excuse me for not having told you the moment it happened? I think I have tried to pretend that he no longer exists — and if he no longer exists then I shouldn't be talking to you about him — but when he materialized in front of me, I fell to pieces.

It has caused me no end of grief. So much grief that I can't even write about it.

After he and I put ourselves through some small talk, I said to him, apropos of nothing but my own shame and hurt feelings: "It was as if you were dead." You know I don't believe in demonic possession, but Jesus, Mary, Mother of God, how ugly the thing that came out of my mouth. His response: raised eyebrows, a bit of a smirk — and I was put on notice that he knew I was trying to get him to go through his paces. One of the publicists came by and made a fuss over the two of us. "Isn't she a love?" she said to Bernard. Bernard, trying to hose down the house fire, said, not without an arch of an eyebrow: "Who doesn't love Frances?"

He was gentleman enough to suggest that I am indeed lovable across all time and by all categories of person when the truth is that I put that fact into serious doubt. His expression meant *I know why you are putting on this show, and you should be scolded for trying to so-*

licit a response, and yet I am going to give it to you, because I did love you once.

He made me wonder if he didn't love me still, but then he cleared that up for me directly. I think I wrote him the bitterest letters I've ever written in my life, and it is making me nauseated every time I remember how bitter those words were. I think I have sinned greatly in being so bitter and in inflicting that bitterness on another.

I haven't been able to concentrate. I was in the middle of a lecture on Orwell yesterday and I stopped to look in the book to find a passage that was going to help me make my point, and when I looked back up at the girls, I couldn't remember where I was or what I had been saying, so I said, "Well, that's enough for today, just go home and work on your final papers," and they all stared at me like they'd just been told their mothers used to skinny-dip. Then they gathered their things and ran out of there, afraid I'd suddenly regain possession of my mind and retract my dismissal.

Claire, maybe I can come out to see you. I've got some money saved, the semester is almost over, Ann's doing fine, and my aunts have offered to look after my father if I want to get out of town. And I do like your friends. It would be nice to talk about the British novel with people who do not think Jane Austen is, and I quote, "a huge snooze." After a while I start to see what these girls mean.

Should I come in the middle of the month?

Love to you and Bill.

Yours,
Frances

January 29, 1963

Dear Claire —

Thank you again for hosting me. It was very cheering to spend time with you and Bill and the rest. Lake Michigan in winter is another proof of God's existence, I think.

The students are status quo. Sometimes there are sniffy principessas but this semester's batch seems to be willing to go along to get along. Thank God. Thank God also I am teaching three courses that I've taught before so I can pretty much draw on previous reserves. Seeing you was a vitamin B shot, but I'm still feeling a little unresponsive to stimuli.

I am sending you pictures of small Alice, as requested. These were taken at Christmas. My favorite is the one where she looks stunned by the tree: *What is this thing you have set me in front of, with its many blinking eyes and drooping whiskers of tinsel?* What you will not see is a picture of her trying to eat the baby Jesus out of Peggy's crèche and the ensuing five-alarm terror. I was the one who took it out of her mouth. Ann wants me to tell you that you are now Alice's honorary aunt, and she thanks you for the clothes you sent back with me.

All my love,
Frances

May 30, 1963

Dear Claire —

I'm sorry I wasn't around yesterday when you called. I'm sorry I haven't responded to your last two letters. I've not been feeling myself.

I guess you know Bernard's new book is out. It's been out since March, I think. I saw it in a bookstore downtown and stood in front of it for a good long minute before I actually opened the cover. They are poems about his loss of faith. I scanned the first few pages but finally could not read them. It was too painful. I felt a possessiveness that I knew was misplaced, and a regret that I knew was not.

I left the store and started crying on the street. I used to see women do this in New York all the time — on the subway, or while I waited in line at Horn and Hardart, and I would always give them a clean handkerchief if I had one — and now I was one of them. Actually, I believe I was, if you will pardon my using so forceful a word, sobbing. There was a church on the corner near the store, and the doors were open, so I walked in and sat down in a pew. I kept sobbing. There was snot coming out of my nose and I did not have a clean handkerchief. I ripped a page out of a missal and made do.

Since then I have been doing a lot of crying for no reason. At my office, in bed, in the kitchen while making dinner. My aunts must know why, because they do not ask what is wrong with me.

I haven't spoken too much about this to you, because I fear it would sound like whining, but I think that what happened with Bernard was a wound that I have not healed from. It hurts too much; it feels like sin. As I sat in that pew, the hurt that had taken root months ago suddenly shot up into a tree that looked like it had been blasted by a storm, its gnarled black branches twisting out faster and faster, the tips of the branches upturned like a hand begging answers from the sky. And no peace being poured into it. Crying in public! Still losing my place in lectures. Losing my place at home. I put my grade book in the freezer and shoved a frozen meat loaf into my school bag, and I didn't notice until I got to campus. I berated my father for forgetting that I am not his wife but his daughter, with Peggy having to take me aside and tell me to get a hold of myself, which was as good as a spanking.

So I sat in the pew and looked at Christ on the cross and spoke to this figure the way I have never spoken to it before: Lord, I am in pain, and I need you to send me a sign that I was right to have never married. Do for me what my aunts claim you have done, day in and day out, for them. I am behaving like a child in my stubborn sadness so I am begging you to treat me like a child who needs signs and wonders to believe in your power. Reward me for never having been a child.

Then Ash Wednesday came, and I understood the psalm in a way I never had before.

> Have mercy on me, O God, according to thy great mercy. And according to the multitude of thy tender mercies blot out my iniquity. For I know my iniquity, and my sin is always before me. To my hearing thou shalt give joy and gladness: and the bones that have been humbled shall rejoice.

So I took up that refrain: If you're not going to give me some spectacular sign, just let me hear of joy and gladness. My sins are too much before me, they are causing an unholy din, so please let me hear of joy and gladness. I can't speak to you respectfully at this moment, so I ask you to open my ears and give me a tune I can follow.

And still it's been all storm, no sign. On Easter Sunday I actually gave myself over to the metaphor of the season. I prayed that God would create a calm heart in me, and that spring would come and I would be as good as new, content in the knowledge that his eye is indeed on the sparrow. But I could tell it wasn't going to take. The lilies at the altar stared at the congregation with a waxiness that seemed even more gauche than usual. The priest seemed even more like a ventriloquist's dummy. Everyone had a look of hazy discomfort, the look you have when you're in a Greyhound station waiting for your hours-late connection. I almost walked out, but out of respect for Ann and my aunts, I stayed put.

Still, I make myself go to Mass. I sit there clinging to the liturgy, letting it climb round me like a vine and keep me in its grip. I am trying not to knock impatiently like one of those virgins locked out of the party but to sit in Mass quietly so I can better hear the words I have heard thousands of times before, and I try to remember to be moved when the wine is held up and we are reminded that this is his blood, which is shed for many unto the forgiveness of sins. Also, I'm exhausted from my own stupidity, so it's about all I can do right now, sit and receive. I like to think of this verse from John: *And I, if I be lifted up from the earth, will draw all things to myself.* There's a sound of mercy ringing through those words, and I am meditating on that. He will draw all people to himself. Even this incredibly bitter one.

That is really all I can hope for. If you know a prayer from a saint that I might carry around with me, please send it.

Love,
Frances

July 1, 1963

Dear Sister Josephine —

I hope you don't mind me writing you when you are visiting your family in Michigan. I hope everyone is well and that you are enjoying the Lake. I've seen it only once in my life, and it made an impression.

I am writing to you because I am in dire need of some spiritual direction. I have never said or written those words to anyone, but I have been experiencing feelings that I know are not right, and I want to find a way to put them behind me. I have not spoken of what I'm about to tell you with my family. Their faith has never wavered. I am 99 percent sure they would tell me to talk to our priest. I have never gone to a priest about anything in my life. I don't think I need to explain to you why.

This is about a person I was in love with and whom I have discovered I am still in love with. I must be, if I am behaving this way.

I have a friend, Claire, whom I have talked to about this, but she has told me only what any friend would tell someone in this situation, which is that he and I were not meant to be. I know she believes this. I try to believe it myself, but I can't. Also, I do not want to burden her any longer with my despair. I know that eventually my despair will exasperate her the way a child's fear of the dark eventually exasperates its parents, and I want to avoid that.

I am writing to you because I believe that you carry a peace within you that is a sign of real faith, and I know from our conversations that you are no stranger to loss. I am experiencing a loss, belatedly, and it has shown me that my faith is flimsier than I'd imagined. And I fear that the real loss I'm mourning here may be the idea of myself as an imperturbable wise child. If you could read this letter and provide some counsel, that would be much appreciated. I am in need of wisdom that is not tainted by the interests of family, friendship, or the Church.

I think I've told you about my friend Bernard. I don't think I've ever mentioned to you that he proposed to me and that I turned him down. Though it killed me to do it, I did not regret it then. Now I am filled with a corrosive, debilitating regret.

I cheated myself out of what might have made me happy, while he seems very happy indeed.

My thoughts are not my own. They are a pot bubbling ferociously with jealousy and rage. I wish I had a reason to go to New York so I could accidentally run into him while wearing a dress that just happened to show me off in a way that would cause Bernard to forget his wife and smuggle me to Paris on the spot. I wish I could write a book that casts his wife as the heroine's foil, a foil the heroine destroys with her wit and virtue to applause from the characters in the book and the critics who review it. I want to write him a letter apologizing for my shortsightedness, which then forces him to write me a letter in which he admits I was the only one he ever loved. I want to write him a letter calling him out on his cowardice in not coming to get me a second time, which then forces him to write me a letter in which he admits I'm the only one he ever loved. I want to write him a letter telling him how beautiful his poems are, which would force him to admit he wrote them all for me. I want to write him a letter telling him how unhappy I am, which would be done in the hopes that he would, for even just a day, be destroyed by the notion that he is the cause of that unhappiness. Just one day. I'm a writer; I could do all those things. I would have art — "Art" — as my excuse. But I'm a Christian, so I could never do any of those things. To do those kinds of things you have to believe in yourself more than you believe in anything else. But I supposedly believe in God more than anything else. And to God, "Art" is never an excuse.

I have never experienced such a derangement of my thoughts. My thoughts, except for a similar episode in college, have mostly been my own. What saved me in college was that I had an unshakable faith in my writing. The story I was truly interested in was the story of myself as a writer, as someone who was going to prove to her family that she did not need to be a mother to be a force for good in the world. So I could very easily put the college boy I was losing in perspective. And this boy very quickly proved himself to have been unworthy of my tears. Things are different now. Now I am thirty, unmarried, living in Philadelphia and not New York, working on a third book that, unlike the first two, feels dead inside. Or maybe it's that I'm dead inside.

Forgive me.

What I have learned about myself is that I have a talent for self-pity. It is like finding that you have a talent for theft, or betrayal. I have learned that I am a Romantic after all, and I have not learned to move to the next stage of first-person suffering, the more noble way of suffering, which would be existentialism and which would have me in a quarrel with the nature of being and time, rather than, like an adolescent, in a quarrel with God, or Bernard. If I were a different kind of writer I would find a way to channel this into a novel. And this is where I am still Romantic — art is a temple, and I shouldn't sully it with my wounded realizations. I think that *great* writers can write to compensate for the losses they endure in real life. I am not sure that I am great. I used to think I might be, but now I'm not so sure. (This, actually, is not the problem. Accepting that I am less than great has been a relief, and I've been writing more because of it.)

I'm a writer — I should find a better way to describe the unrelenting pain I'm in, but I'm in pain, and my creative faculties are dulled. This hurt has been more destructive than the hurt I experienced watching my father fade away from us into senility. And for that I'm ashamed. There was some rage there when I saw my father failing and would not admit to myself what was happening, but it is different from the rage I direct toward myself because I made a mistake. Or the rage I direct toward Bernard for not allowing me to have some contact with him still.

Oh, Sister. There is a lot of anger in this letter. I may not even be making any sense. Forgive me.

You may have noticed that I have not mentioned God much in this letter. This is the problem. I will sit in Mass, sit in pews, trying to stop the flow of feelings, but those feelings — have you ever seen pictures of a squid letting loose its ink in the ocean? That's what I feel like. I put myself in the pew, I say God's name, but he is blotted out by a rapidly issuing cloud of the blackest thoughts. I thought God was the one who told me to refuse Bernard — I went to St. Patrick's for two weeks straight and rose up from the paddocks thinking I'd been given direction. And now I wonder. I used to believe in his mercy and that maybe suffering was a form of his mercy. Not anymore. Some of us have a talent for suffering — but I guess I don't. What is the point of God if he cannot soothe us? What is the point of believing in something all-powerful if he cannot give you the strength to go on at this very moment? What is the point of other people if you cannot keep your hands on them? I refuse to think, as my aunts might suggest, that these are God-given lessons. That just makes God a scold, and I refuse to believe that he is.

And then I am dismayed at the very adolescent nature of these objections. This is all I could come up with? I must really be losing my mind. Also, I am a hypocrite. I once warned Bernard about becoming God's disgruntled customer, and here I am.

Sister, I thank you if you can read even a quarter of this. Now you know what it is like to have a teenage daughter. You must have thought you were escaping this through the convent. My sincere apologies.

Yours,
Frances

July 1, 1963

Frances —

Hello! I hope this letter finds you and your family well.

I know it must be strange for you to hear from me, since it has been years since we've spoken, but I saw your most recent book in the windows of the bookstore in Harvard Square, went in and bought it, started to read it that night, finished it the next day, and I have been thinking of you ever since. The book is terrific. Kudos. You know I've stopped reading current fiction — once I headed for law school, I decided that I would read only history, biography, reportage, and political thought, and I have never felt anything remotely like a hole in my soul since, which means that I was right to give up writing for lawyering. Maybe once a year I'll read *Our Mutual Friend,* when Kay and I go to Maine, but that's it. From what I remember, current fiction used to be pretty insipid, and I'm betting it's pretty insipid now too. But your book is fantastic. Every sentence is a whip crack.

Reading your book made me think that it's about time I got something off my chest, and that maybe you could take it. I'm well aware that what I'm about to write could make you angry, because it's betraying someone's confidence and would assume a certain amount of lingering feelings on your part. You might understandably take offense at someone assuming you've got even two drops of regret over Bernard.

Bernard told me what happened between you two last fall. He was pretty torn up about it. I told him that he shouldn't have engaged you. You shouldn't have engaged with a married man either. I'm not saying it's wrong, I'm just saying it's wrong for you. I don't think you have the constitution. I can just imagine your Catholic blood boiling over that bit of amoral reasoning. But I do believe that what he wrote you afterward — at least, what he told me he wrote you — came out of a real struggle with his conscience. He was not toying with you.

Let me get to the point of why I'm writing. If you do have any lingering feelings of regret about not marrying Bernard, you should not. He tries to be faithful to Susan, and I think he does love her, but he's fooled with one girl a year for every year of their marriage. These girls are notable only for their conventional prettiness (they wear very tiny hair bows, I've noticed) and their lack of wit. It's a little embarrassing how indistinguishable they are from each other, and it's a little embarrassing how they resemble you (physically) more than they resemble Susan. It happens every spring. It predicts every hospital visit. He gets a girl in his cross hairs, usually a student; he starts coming home late, and sometimes not at all. Three months later, he's in the hospital, and Susan has to tell the girl to go home, he can't come out to play. He might have told you this, in which case I'll tell you this again so that he's corroborated. What he might not have told you but that you might have heard is that Susan has had to, at least once that I know of, plead his case in front of the president of Columbia University to keep him from being fired.

At one point I thought that you were the only one for him, but now I think you were lucky. You wouldn't have been his wife; you would have been a game warden. Even I was blinded to the reality of what life with Bernard would be. And I'd picked him up off bar floors and kept him from fights. I should have known better than to cheer the both of you on. But I'd been picked up from bar floors by him as often as he'd been picked up by me, so I thought his big stupid heart and his big stupid generosity would make up for his insanity. All the sentimentalism I've spent my life trying to hide broke out on me like a big red pimple at the sight of you two together. I was actually peeved when he proposed to Susan, and she could tell. Now I silently ask her forgiveness whenever I see her and she seems not to want to shoot me. But Susan never had anything in her that needed protecting from Bernard. There's no art in her. Take it from someone who doesn't have any art in himself, either. If this were 1914, she would be a war nurse. Things being what they are in 19-whatever-this-is, with you ladies able to do pretty much what you damn please without being forced into the convent in order to exercise your minds, she married Bernard.

You were right not to marry him but he won't ever love anyone the way he loved you. He can't tell you this, and he shouldn't tell you this, so I will.

Ever yours,
Ted

October 5, 1963

Dear Ted —

Thank you so very much for your letter. I was not offended. I was grateful. It's a long story, but it came at just the right time. It saved me from sending one to another friend, one that I might have been sorry to have signed my name to. As an atheist, would you be offended if I said that your letter might have been an answer to prayer?

I don't know what to say, exactly, to your letter — this is why it's taken me a little while to write back to you. I have decided that I don't feel comfortable saying much other than I am grateful for your candor. I think in this position a lady should keep the many thoughts and feelings occasioned by such a letter to herself and just try to make it clear that she is grateful. I hope you understand. You sound buoyant, as usual, and that makes me happy. Thank you also for reading my book. You know I feel the same way about Current Fiction, so your praise means a great deal to me.

If you ever find yourself in Philadelphia, please do let me know. It would be my honor to stand you a drink. My greetings to Kay.

With love,
Frances

March 20, 1964

Dear Claire —

You sneaky Claire. Thank you for sending me the Julia Child book for my birthday. I have been circling it like a hawk — well, a slightly intimidated hawk, if such a thing exists — ever since it was published, but now that I have it there are going to be no more excuses. It is time now to Contend with the French.

This seems to be a theme lately. I have been seeing a gentleman from France. A professor at Penn. Of French literature. I think it's a joke, actually, that I am seeing a gentleman from France, but we get on, and keep getting on. His name is — I can't write it, as it seems like a joke too, a parody of the echt-French. Like Jean Valjean. Or Jean-Luc Godard. Or Pepé Le Pew. I'll write it: his name is Alain. I can't say his name aloud. If we keep seeing each other, I am going to have to figure out how to avoid addressing him by his Christian name. Nevertheless, we have been to the cinema, the cinema again, to the cinema one more time, and to Fairmount Park. I have started to wonder if God does indeed give us gifts other than the gift of forbearance.

I apologize for not having told you this immediately — one would think that, with you and I having been friends for so many years, I'd know by now that you don't mind anything I tell you, but I wasn't sure if it would pan out into anything worth mentioning.

I met him at a lecture at Penn. I took a copy of *Story of a Soul* with me — I've been reading it for this talk I have to give next month. He was sitting next to me, and I noticed that he seemed to be looking at the book before the lecture started. When I got up he said, "Excuse me, miss." *Meese.* "Is that Saint Thérèse you're reading?" I said yes, and he said, "Do you love her?" I heard the accent. He had the face I always associate with the echt-French — olive-skinned; slight flush to the cheeks; horizontal, heavy black brows; long nose. The kind I always imagine will pucker into some mocking impression of my sickly accent or my cheap plastic American sunglasses.

I was a little taken aback — the question must have meant that he loved her, and my answer was going to be less enthusiastic than he might have hoped for. "May I say that I'm not sure?" I said. He laughed.

"Do you love her?" I said. "Oh yes, I do," he said. "It's not fashionable at all, and I keep it a secret from my colleagues. She's the kind of girl Balzac would punish for her innocence by sending her to Paris and turning her into a corrupt chorus girl." I laughed.

"Do you know she wrote poems?" he asked. No, I said. "If any young man writes you poems like Saint Thérèse, you must marry him. They're quite passionate."

I think he interpreted the look on my face as meaning he'd said the wrong thing, but that wasn't it — really, I was trying not to laugh. *"Pardonnez"* — he began — "pardon me," he ended. Did he want to get a coffee? He did.

I have learned to like my solitude, but I like his company just as much — if not more. He laughs with pure delight much more than I imagined the French would — I guess this would be the part of the French soul responsible for champagne? And yet I have not spoken a word of French to him. I dare not.

Everyone sends love.

xx

Frances

September 5, 1965

F —

Bill and I say it's official: you have won a prize. And your aunts dote on him like the Vatican sent him. I doubt Helen will ever call him anything other than Allen. Poor guy. Please tell Peggy that we were devastated to get to the end of the lunch she packed us for the drive home. Bill sends his love.

Frances, I have to tell you I was worried that you felt the need to settle. When you first wrote me about Alain, I didn't think you were really going to fall in love with him. You seemed more bemused than smitten. I had a fear that you were going to drift into something that looked perfectly sensible to everyone around you — so bloody sensible that you'd never argue yourself out of it, and you'd just pull him over you like a blanket and go to sleep. It's unfair, I know, but I often thought that only your being pursued by Gregory Peck would have put my worries at ease.

What's also unfair is that I wanted marriage for you only because I myself could not tumble along without it. You never did hanker after it the way I did, so why should I be anxious for you if your life was leading you places other than the altar? My job is a party I go to every day. I need to be in the middle of a commotion that isn't children, and the paper is exactly that and no more. And then I have Bill, my roaring home fire. You rely on your books for things the rest of us search for in people. I don't think that's a bad thing. I think it's a gift, maybe even your one true spiritual discipline. Go ahead, roll your eyes.

Whenever you talked about marrying Bernard, you had trepidation rumbling through you like an earthquake tremor. I had the feeling that if you did marry him, your sister's shotgun marriage would have been happier than your freely chosen one, and that was an irony I did not want to have to watch deepen over the years. But I don't see any of that when you talk of marrying A., and I don't think it's because you've been cutting deals with yourself. He's very funny and he's very wise. What was it you said he told you? "Your books need no help from me. They are for you alone." If a man has no delusions about what he is going to be to you — and you have no delusions about what you need from him — it may be that you have a true love on your hands.

Why haven't I said these things to you before? You didn't need me poking around where you were sore. And I thought the right thing to do was to keep quiet, because deep down, I trusted you to do whatever was right for you. Which you did. To that I say cheers, and drink up.

All my happiest love,
C

April 20, 1966

Dear Ted —

So, that award ceremony. It left me sadder than I imagined it would. I was sadder than I thought I would be even upon seeing her. I notice, the older I get, that the sadness is coming in regularly like the tides, eroding my reserves of joy. My illness has done nothing to help this. Some days, it's not so terrible. I feel like those dinosaurs in the natural history museum, viewed with Bess on my hand: stripped bare of defenses, ready to collapse into an incoherent meaningless heap should someone jounce it the wrong way, but somehow still standing, with a few props, and in its suggested outline still a thing to stand under and wonder at. I feel this way most often when I am in front of the students. They are paying to find wisdom at the feet of an elder. Mostly they are good, serious children. If they rubberneck, it's in spite of themselves. I can see one girl, the best student this semester, looking away from me when she talks to me during office hours; she keeps her hands in her lap, speaks very quickly, forgets her coat or bag when she leaves, and I am fairly sure it's because she's heard I might put my hand up her dress, though she doesn't want to believe it — she wants to think I am a noncorporeal oracle uncle interested only in poetry, but she knows she has to act on what might be lore in order to get home safe and not be accused of being a bewitcher herself. It's touching to see her struggle — she is willing to go into the monster's cave in order to clarify her thoughts on the freeing of verse. And I can't say anything without damning myself to assure her she's safe, and that she's safe because she looks like Susan.

All the men I know come out of their offices rubbing their faces, looking as if they have just been unceremoniously roused from sleep. Each wife's face is fallen and crumpled into a spider web of worry lines. Everyone looks at each other sidelong, exhausted, refusing to name the things that nail them down. I wish they would, though. I long ago decided psychoanalysis was not a long-term solution, but I do think everyone needs a talking cure now and then, especially if it's administered by a sympathetic layperson. Even the people I used to count on to throw depth charges into the state of things prefer to steer clear of that adventure. Truth be told, it's no longer an adventure — it's more of an inventory of an increasingly empty larder. The other night I was out with Russell and when, after the drinks had been set down before us, I asked, in all sincerity, "How are you?" he looked at me with befuddled scorn and said, "We're here to talk about my book."

I am glad that Frances won this award. I didn't read this last book, and I won't, and I don't think I will read the next ones, but I am still proud of her. I took a look at the first sentence and saw she was still able to tack into the wind with a sure hand. That's all I wanted to know.

Her husband — a professor — appears to be an intelligent man. I still can't quite believe she married a Frenchman. I suppose I always imagined Frances much too American, and much too committed to the culture of her own idiosyncrasies, to marry someone who would continuously force her into possibly destabilizing acts of translation. After we filed out of the auditorium, he shook my hand with confidence. Not prurience. She stood next to him with her hands clasped behind her back as he did so. She did not show him any more affection than she showed me when we were in a public place. I did not want to be relieved about this, but I was.

We were able to stand near each other smiling for the photographs. Near, and not next to, because she put another poet and a playwright between us. While the pictures were being taken, Susan went to the restaurant ahead of us, I think so she would not have to see how I would respond to Frances's presence. But neither of us was interested in being alone with each other. There was nothing left to say.

To think we might have been standing together in another ceremony entirely. But here we are as ghosts to each other, the sight of the other stirring nothing but skittishness. I saw her enter the building and I tucked my head down, pretending that I needed something from my wallet. When we were finally forced to speak, I touched her arm and she pulled away.

This is what the world asks of us — to move about as the dead as penance for having dwelt in an improbable passion. The metaphors for love — metaphors of illness, of madness. In this way we pardon ourselves for our lapses in duty, hoping that no one will ever disparage us by saying that we were not sufficiently contented by the world as it is. But love is another law, too, and it will judge you if you do not bend to it when it asks. I think it has already judged her, and now it is judging me.

I hear Susan ribbing me as I write for, as she likes to say, turning tubercular with sentiment like Keats — whenever I mourn the breaking up of a pair of my students for whatever reason, Susan clucks her tongue at me. It's better that they learn now that it's silly to fall so hard, she'll say. They've gotten it out of their systems and next time they'll be wiser. Or if I speak without censure of friends or acquaintances who find themselves in adulterous positions, if I try to have sympathy for both parties — so long, of course, as both parties have not done anything vindictive — she'll accuse me of being a moral relativist. (Whenever she says this, I have to bite my tongue to keep from repeating to her your theory that if a woman accuses an adulterer of moral relativism, it's because she was never considered worth an affair in the first place.) She may also think that my sympathy with the romantically confounded is my madness at its lowest boil.

Sometimes I will see a girl on campus, or in the back of class, who has the look of one of the episodic girls. On those days, when I feel that I am Bluebeard sensing the blood pooling behind lock and key, pooling and about to creep out from under the door, I will find a confessional at my earliest convenience. A formality, but one I am glad to submit to when I cannot convince myself I am a man who means well, at least when I am sane. That's about as far as I can go these days in giving myself credit. I leave it to Bess to make more of me than I am.

I don't blame Susan — I blame myself for not having the courage to leave her. I think she knows that my staying with her is an attempt at atonement. Even as I say I don't believe, I see that my higher law, when it cannot be love, is God, whose law demands self-sacrifice. It's a form I can submit to. Even in my poetry, I cannot escape submitting to form.

After the dinner, I did what a responsible husband would do, which was to drink a great deal with other people in order to forget she ever happened and to present back at home a fulfilled and dedicated heart to my wife. If Frances is someone I will have to spend my life occasionally drinking to forget, that seems like too fair a bargain.

Bernard

June 11, 1968

Dear Bernard —

It has been a very long time. I hope you don't mind my writing. John sent me your new book — I asked for it — and I felt moved to write to say how very much I enjoyed it. "For Bess" especially. The last two lines have followed me around for the past week or so. John might have told you, but I have a daughter now. She's almost nine months old, and her name is Katherine, after my mother. I have read her your poem several times, and she approves.

I don't expect that you'll answer this letter. I'll understand if you don't.

My best to you.

Sincerely,
Frances

September 20, 1968

Dear Frances —

Thank you for your note. It tumbled out of a pile of mail I was picking up during some harried office hours, and I couldn't have been happier to see your name on the left-hand corner of the envelope.

Congratulations on your Katherine. John did mention her arrival to me. I think God has favored us by giving us daughters. They are music in the house.

That poem was for Bess, but it was also for you. I had been wanting to write you a letter but couldn't. It turned into a poem.

Keep me in your prayers, won't you?

Yours,
Bernard

ACKNOWLEDGMENTS

It is my incredible good fortune to have had PJ Mark and Jenna Johnson believing in this book the way they did, and thinking as hard about it with me as if it were their own. My gratitude to PJ for his early enthusiasm and his assiduous, astute readings; my gratitude to Jenna for editing me with an exceedingly sharp and imaginative eye, and for her indefatigable faith, hope, and verve. I am very lucky to have both of them on my side.

I can't thank Houghton Mifflin Harcourt enough for their support of this book—especially Elizabeth Anderson, Carla Gray, Summer Smith, and Lori Glazer. I salute copyeditor Tracy Roe and executive manuscript editor Larry Cooper because they are exemplars of their craft.

Many, many thanks to Donna Freitas and Lauren Sandler for their crucial (and passionate!) insights.

Thanks also to Mary Ann Naples, who told me to keep going.

And to Dan and Ilona McGuiness, for teaching me more than writing.

As always, I owe more than I can say to my parents, my sister, and Mr. John Williams, who has redefined the word gentleman for the twenty-first century.